NECROMANCER

A NOVEL

EDDIE ROY

Copyright ©2025 by Eddie Roy.

ISBN 978-1-966540-18-2 (softcover)
ISBN 978-1-966540-19-9 (ebook)

All rights reserved. No part of this book may be reproduced or transmitted in any form or by any means, electronic or mechanical, including photocopying, recording, or by any information storage and retrieval system without express written permission from the author, except in the case of brief quotations embodied in critical reviews and certain other non-commercial uses permitted by copyright law.

This book is a work of fiction. Names, characters, places, and incidents are the product of the author's imagination or are used fictitiously. Any resemblance to actual locales, events, or persons, living or dead, is purely coincidental.

Printed in the United States of America.

NECROMANCER

A NOVEL

EDDIE ROY

We battle not against flesh and blood,
but against forces and rulers of darkness
and the spiritual powers of evil.

—Ephesians 6:12

PATTY LOST

David Boyd opened his eyes at the rattling growl of the garbage truck circling the cul-de-sac that lay like an asphalt crop circle in front of his house. He'd lived in the vinyl-sided cracker box house for more than eight years. It was one of the oldest in the development, ten minutes east of Boise. The builders had broken ground for the development's first house a little less than ten years before. His house was at the end of the cul-de-sac, and the old rattle-trap trash truck paused in mid turn-around to pick up his cans; well only one can now. Since he was alone in the house, he created less garbage; most of it being beer cans, vodka bottles and carryout fast-food bags. The washing machine hadn't been turned on in two months. Thanks to the advance royalty check he'd received from the record company just three weeks before, he could afford to buy new clothes every day, but he didn't. He might have gotten enjoyment out of the experience; enjoyment he didn't deserve.

Patty happened to be sitting at the side of the road. She'd been waiting for AAA to send someone to change a flat tire. At the same, time a trucker who'd been traveling on reds and caffeine for twenty-six hours finally lost his battle with sleep and rear-ended her little Ford Focus. The car flew fifty yards and landed upside down across the median and slid into oncoming traffic, like an out-of-control turtle on its back. It didn't burn, but the sun roof was open, and when the firemen who responded jacked the car up enough for the EMTs to look under it, the lower half of Patty's body was still in the car, but when the car flipped, she'd been thrown halfway out of the sun-roof. Above her waist she was simply gone. What was left of the car looked like a toy some kid had dragged back and forth over a rough sidewalk. It had all been a case of her being in the wrong place at the wrong time.

Still, David felt responsible, and that feeling nearly crushed his capacity to care about anything. He'd made excuses when she asked him to go to the grocery store with her. If he'd been there to change the tire, they'd have been together somewhere else, instead of her sitting alone on the shoulder of the road when the truck driver's head dropped to his steering wheel. He still could barely force himself to eat, or do laundry. He'd picked up some jeans and t-shirts at a Salvation-Army thrift store that were close to his size, and rinsed them out in the bathroom sink when they needed it. He hung them on the shower curtain rod to dry. The sound of the washing machine would have driven him mad. He wouldn't have been able to help looking in the laundry room whenever he walked past. He knew that not seeing Patty folding clothes; with the sweet smell of fabric softener filling the room, would be more than he could handle. With the advance check, he could have bought them both new clothes every day, but he didn't. No, he couldn't. He had been holding onto the money to buy her an engagement ring. It was more money than they'd ever had in the ten years they'd been together, and he'd wanted the ring to be something special. He hadn't proposed, wanting to have the ring when he did. She died without knowing he'd planned on making an honest woman of her. He finally bought the ring anyway, after she was gone and wore it on a chain around his neck. It was the only thing he could think of to keep her with him; the ring and, of course, Davey.

When he was Noose, the alter ego he became on stage, before the grief drove him into self-imposed exile, the ring still hung around his neck: but he swung it around so it lay against his back. He didn't want it touching the black steel pentagram that had become such a part of his stage persona. It was all part of the death-metal shtick, as was the gallows behind them on stage. They were expected to live up to the death part of death-metal; at least in image. The phrase stuck in his head, every time it came to him; 'live up to the death'. It had the ring of something that would be right at home printed in a Hallmark card, if Ozzy Osbourne wrote their jingles.

It was all a game he'd played, seemingly forever, but only seemingly. He could barely recall the time when he was proud of his music. His life had changed on his eleventh birthday; the day his grandfather gave him his first guitar. He wasn't really surprised at the gift, it was something he'd been asking for ever since a neighbor, who was a musician, played him an Eric Clapton CD during a trip to a local music store. But surprise or not, it was the most amazing gift he'd ever gotten; but it wasn't Noose who spent every waking hour practicing back then. It was David. It had taken seemingly forever for his friends to talk him back onto the stage after losing Patty. Virtually without fail, everyone he talked to urged him to play; even his mother, who had insisted on taking care of Davey after Patty's death.

It was Davey that had made him realize the importance of finding his way back into a reality that didn't include living in the darkest abyss he could find. What had started as a stage gimmick, no more real than Alice Coopers' guillotine, had gradually gotten a hold on him. Every time he picked up the guitar, the irony hit him. It was something he rarely thought about when he'd had Patty to focus on. He couldn't escape the irony of his being in a death-metal band from Boise, Idaho, of all places; a band that appeared ready to make it big.

David and Patty met about a year and a half after his creative desperation guided him in a direction he would eventually recognize as the beginning of his downward spiral. They met at a party in a hotel room after a Sunday night '*Corpse Whisperer*' show. It hadn't taken long from the formation of the band for David to wish he'd found something different. Like most after-show parties, it soon became more riot than party. At first nobody got violent or completely out of control. But more than a few of the band's hangers-on got wasted and started playing to the crowd. One freak with pentagrams tattooed on his eyelids started pushing people around and groping every female in the room. David didn't know the guy, and immediately didn't like him. It wasn't long before he tired of the asshole's antics. The guy had several of the chicks giggling and ready to jump in the sack. They were as wasted as he was. As always, there were girls around who would do anything to be with a musician. It could be any musician, from any band. Or in this case, any band's party. It was an immutable fact; true from the biggest metal bands; playing stadiums, to backwoods hillbilly bands in bars decorated with moose heads and wagon wheels.

But that night, in that hotel room, David walked in the bathroom and found the wasted asshole holding a beautiful girl's head under the running sink faucet. She was choking and crying at the same time. The sound combination was more than David could stand. He went back into the room and came in with a half full vodka bottle and hit the guy in the temple so hard his head spun around almost a far as had Linda Blair's in "The Exorcist".

His intention was to save the drowning girl, which he did. He had no idea what else he'd done till four days later when he sat in an office in the Boise headquarters of the FBI: something he'd never known existed. An FBI agent sat across from him, whispering conspiratorially. It wasn't their first meeting. The first had been the night he nailed the guy with the vodka bottle. By the time the Boise police arrived on the scene, the guy he'd hit smashed the bathroom window and disappeared down an alley behind the hotel, leaving a substantial trail of blood. The girl David saved got a look at the guy before he went out the window and said David's blow with the bottle had opened a gash over one eye so severe that a flap of bloody skin hung over his eye like an extra, inside-out eye lid. So, the police didn't know if the blood was from the gash or from the broken window glass; not that it mattered; either way the blood gave them a place to start. The agent whispered to minimize the shock of what he was about to say. He introduced himself as Special Agent John Paxton. He began by praising David for stepping in when he saw the girl being drowned in the hotel bathroom. Then he told him the rest of the story, as Paul Harvey used to say. "David, we got a D.N.A. hit on the blood the perp left behind. You know what perp means?"

"Yeah, I watch TV. Who is he?"

"We don't have an ID yet, he's not in any database, but we did match his D.N.A. to samples from three other crime scenes. You did more good than you know."

"How's that?" David inquired, bewildered.

"The other samples were from a murder and two rape/beatings. One of his victims has been a coma for the past three months. The doctor's conclusion was that he tried to rape her, but couldn't get it up, so he beat her instead. The D.N.A. sample was from saliva. Either he spit on her, or drooled on her. Since he couldn't show her who was in control by raping her, he showed it by beating her. That shit happens more than you'd believe. Sometimes I wonder if we should start giving the freaks and perverts Viagra. Getting a hard-on and raping somebody is better than not getting one and beating her to death. There's a good chance she'll never come out of it. This is a very bad guy, and there's no telling how many future victims you saved. We followed his blood trail till it stopped in a parking lot. There was a big puddle by one of the end spaces, where he must have stood still long enough to open a car door. When he backed from the space, one of his tires rolled through the blood. We're hoping the tread pattern will help track down the car."

"That's all you've got to go on?"

"Right now, but I almost hope it doesn't pay off. Finding him would be great; it would prevent him from hurting anyone else. But it's not my first choice."

"What's your first choice?" David asked; honestly curious.

"I can't say this officially, but I hope the bastard dies a painful death from blood poisoning. Or, even better: lead poisoning. Especially if I'm the one who puts the lead in him"

David narrowed his eyes and silently stared across the table at Paxton.

"What?"

David smiled a small tight-lipped smile that held absolutely no humor and said, "Now I know why you're a Special Agent."

Despite all the horror involved in the situation, the silver lining was falling in love with the girl he'd saved: Patty. Less than three months later they moved in together. A few months after that, they'd bought the house; a move toward the normalcy David thought he had lost all chances at, after the craziness that came with the death-metal. Patty came into his life at exactly the right time to save him, just as he'd come into the hotel bathroom at the right time to save her. Buying the house was a leap of faith. She'd been out of work for over a year, since the company she worked for downsized during the recession. 'Corpse Whisperer' was getting to be known in and around Boise, but if you mentioned the name a hundred miles from the city, nobody had a clue who or what you were talking about. He wouldn't have taken on the responsibility that came with the little house if not for Patty's positive outlook on life. She once told him while they lay in bed watching one of her chick flicks that she knew nothing could go wrong. If things weren't supposed to go right for them, he wouldn't have walked into the hotel bathroom when he did. He'd just smiled at her and said she must be right; they were meant to be together, or he wouldn't be watching a Julia Roberts movie while his leather and chains stage costume was draped across the foot-board of the bed. The contrast was crazy, but crazy didn't bother him when he was with her.

Thirteen months after that, Davey was born. He was born two weeks early and didn't weigh what the doctor hoped he would, but other than not wanting to latch on when Patty tried to get him to breast-feed, he was perfect. David had asked, "Are you sure he's mine? I never had to be talked into that. Do you think I should show him how?"

"How do you know you didn't need to be talked into it? Why don't you call your mother and ask how you did when you were twenty-four hours old."

"I don't think so."

"You want me to ask her?" Patty asked shyly.

"Do you want to die young?" David had asked in a mocking tone, unaware that less than eight months later he would be burying the half of her that stayed in the car.

Still, the second-best thing that ever happened to him had happened, even if Davey didn't realize the value of a nipple.

Then the reality hit like a sledgehammer; Patty was gone, and he was left with the responsibility of caring for another human being; one that was half Patty.

David knew he was about as qualified to raise a child as he was to pilot a space shuttle or perform open heart surgery.

He was a guitarist, for God's sake. And not even a really good one. Just loud, and able to put together a string of words on a page to scream. He thought he remembered hearing that one of The Beatles said "Once the show starts, and the crowd starts, we can't hear anything. Or maybe it was Pete Townshend? He couldn't recall. They wouldn't have had to tune their guitars or even turn the mikes on. The crowd was there to scream and party; they were part of the show. The band on stage was only background noise. Just like the asphalt oval was just there to justify the partying at a NASCAR race, between crashes. Or an NFL game was a good reason to tailgate; as good a reason as any.

People needed a break from their own reality; like the guy who climbs in a yellow car every day and hauls people around. Many of them pay him to drive them two blocks. A big portion of them were business drones that desperately need the exercise of a measly two block walk. People who earn as much in the time it took him to drive the two blocks as he'll make in a week. That's the reality one man wants; no needs, to escape.

David understood and appreciated the realities from which people needed to escape. At one time, he'd been happy, at least for a while, to provide their background noise. Back then, the background noise, while it wouldn't always fit the soundtrack of a Disney movie about bunnies or butterflies, was noise meant only to be enjoyed, to entertain. The death-metal was very different; it was designed to glorify darkness. Both outer darkness and the darkness people carried inside. But the music brought with it what every musician wants; adoration. Any musician, famous or not, revels in the response of the crowd. Standing on stage, while people scream and clap and yell your name is addictive. David was addicted. He hated the music and the life, but he was addicted to the applause. Then Patty was gone; in the blink of an eye. And he was left to be a father; ready or not.

So, all he had left was an engagement ring he'd never given Patty, and the son she'd given him. He could put the ring in a drawer, push the drawer closed and pray he'd forget it was there. He wanted to forget the ring, but not who he'd bought it for. So as David stood in the bedroom of the cracker-box house that had been a home, *their* home, and listened to the rattle and groan of the garbage truck stopping at his little slice of the pie that was the cul-de-sac outside in the world he'd decided to hide from, and being afraid to put his clothes in the washer, because the smell of the laundry detergent would make Patty's ghost appear in his mind, leaning against the washer, and reaching for the drier sheets on the high shelf above the machine. He had no concept of the horror coming his way.

His first response when his friends and band mates started hounding him to go back on stage had been a loud and unapologetically rude; 'Hell no!' Then they had started the wearing-down process. Everything from; Patty would want you to, to make it a tribute in her honor. But the one that actually, instead of swaying him toward their way of thinking, gave him a huge reason to stay far away from his guitar and the clubs came from his drummer, Phil Russell, who at his best (stone cold sober) was a total burn-out. He innocently said, "David, maybe the music will be cathartic, you know; cleansing, maybe help you forget.

Even beyond David's amazement at the drummer using the word "cathartic", the statement made him totally furious. David grabbed the man, who outweighed him by at least twenty-five pounds and gave his best effort at shaking him. The bulk of the drummer barely moved, and David managed only to shake himself violently. He finally gave up on shaking and yelled in the drummer's face, "Are you fuckin' nuts? I'm going through the worst hurt of my life. I buried my fiancé eight days ago, and you think going on stage and screaming about death, murder, suicide, and burning in hell for two hours is going to make me forget my troubles?"

"Well, when you put it that way it does sound kinda' dumb," Phil mumbled. Ed Jones, the bass player, who'd been standing six feet or so away, leaning on a stack of amps, said, "Way more than kinda', you idiot." But finally, he had gone on stage, and it wasn't cathartic, or cleansing. What the fuck it was he couldn't name. But it wasn't a tribute to Patty, no matter how hard he tried to justify it in his mind. And he was certain that despite how everyone tried to convince him differently, he knew it wasn't what Patty would have wanted. She wouldn't want him to be miserable, but she also wouldn't want him to go back to preaching death.

Unbelievably, the one who'd finally cleared his head enough for him to think reasonably, if not wisely, and directed him back to the stage; directed, not pushed, was his mother. His whole life, he'd known she was the one to talk to when he needed to be slapped into reality. He once told her that she should have whatever it was that she had put in bottles, and label it "No Smoke Up Your Ass Concentrate". Just add water and drink as needed in times of extreme confusion". "Also helpful for moderate to severe-stupidity". Every cure on TV these days was for moderate to severe something. So, it only seemed logical that Mom's concentrate should be targeted at moderate to severe stupidity.

As always, she'd put things clearly and succinctly; And while she agreed that Patty wouldn't want him on stage promoting a lifestyle with a center core of hatred and death; She was just as certain that Patty wouldn't want him to curl up in a ball and gradually cease to exist. He needed to exist. She told him about a conversation she and Patty had once had, soon after Davey's birth. Patty had said, "Sometimes I wonder if the only reason I ever existed was to be where I was at just that exact time, so David could save me, and no telling how many others." "So?" David asked, "You think God, or whoever created Patty just to be drowning under a faucet in a hotel bathroom, so I could nail a stoner with a bottle? You really believe that? That He would torture her that way, just to teach a lesson. So, he could put her bust on the shelf of misery, right beside the one of Job. "I'm not sure what I believe," his mother said softly. Then, her voice barely a breath, said. "But Patty believed it." Then, in her more normal motherly voice, she said, "Patty believed her only reason for being was to bring out your goodness, and to aim you toward a more normal life. Don't disappoint her."

So, David went on stage. The rest of the band members were ecstatic. They all, of course, asked what changed his mind. He never gave an answer. He simply smiled a small, thin smile; empty of humor, and let them guess for themselves. If he tried to explain, it would be a mistake. He could never put it into words. He really couldn't understand himself. Patty had hated the death-metal, even more than he did. But she never pushed. She gave him time and space to decide where to go and what to do. Then she died; chewed up like she'd been in a food processor. She'd lived long enough to give him a shove in the right direction. And to give him Davey; a reason to keep him going in the right direction. But he would have to stay on the correct road on his own. On his own he'd never be what Danny needed and deserved. So, his mother had taken Davey. David knew as well as she did; it was the right thing to do. She knew how to be a mother. David had not a clue how to be a father. So, knowing Davey was safe, well-loved, and well cared for, he went back on stage. The ring Patty never even saw hung on a chain around his neck, but swung around on his back, to be certain it would never touch the pentagram that hung on his chest. He made sure to see Davey every day, and talked to him as he lay in his bassinet, even before the boy was familiar enough with him to smile whenever he came in. Sometimes he talked for hours, with his throat raw from what passed for singing in *Corpse Whisperer*. He talked about Patty, and told Davey what a great mom she would have been. He talked about how someday they'd go for walks in the park. On those walks,

Davey would sit on his shoulders and look around. They'd be sure to do it in the fall, when the leaves had turned, and the woods looked almost like they were on fire with the colors. He told him that when he was old enough, maybe they'd get a puppy, a rescue dog. They were always the best. And every one of them needed a savior. A savior to save them a visit; their last visit. A visit to a gas chamber or a needle that shot cold liquid into an unsuspecting vein. The one they'd pick out might not be the cutest or the smartest. They'd choose the one that seemed to need a master as much as they needed a dog. Male or female wouldn't matter either. They'd know the perfect dog at first sight. But it would have been a lot more fun with Patty along. She was always a good judge of character. And he promised Davey that when he was big enough, they'd play in the leaves together. The three of them; David, his son and their dog, that Davey would name. He felt every boy should name his own dog.

As David talked, Davey would lie there in the bassinet, smiling and making cooing sounds, and once in a while bursting out with what could only be a real laugh. Davey always looked up at him, listening intently to words he didn't understand, and when he smiled, David's heart leapt and sank at the same time. When he smiled, it was like someone had taken Patty's smile and painted it on his face. David never wore his stage regalia when he visited Davey. That false persona was a side of him he never wanted Davey to see. And once in a while, when he said just the right thing, and made Davey laugh, he thought, 'Maybe I really could be a dad.' And for a little while he felt like the David Patty had wanted him to be. And for a little while he felt good about himself.

Now, as he stood in the bedroom, listening to the garbage truck lumber away, carrying the leftovers of what his life had become, all those memories had come flooding in, like a movie first running backwards to the moment he heard Patty choking and crying under the hotel faucet. Then running forward again to this moment, standing alone in the bedroom, trying to decide what to do with this, just another day.

The sound of pounding at his front door shook him from his reverie. He blinked once, then again, to squeeze the tears from his eyes. He didn't bother to wipe them away when they ran down his cheeks. He felt he owned them, and didn't think Patty would mind. The memories had brought both tears of loss and of joy, and he figured fifty percent was the best he could hope for. And if that was the best, he could live with it. Then the pounding came again, loud and insistent. Though he wasn't in the mood for visitors, he shuffled to the door. Then he learned that no matter where you are, or how miserable your life is, there's always room for more misery. Why was it that in a world where there are people starving for lack of food, or dying for lack of a simple injection, or with no clothes, or no home? In a world where there were so many things that there's never enough of, why was misery always in such plentiful supply? While people are starving, there was always so much misery; it was like an all-you-can-suffer buffet.

DAVEY LOST

David could have guessed for years and still not have guessed who was on the other side of the door. Even though he'd met the person knocking before; in fact, had had more than one meeting with him, David still didn't immediately recognize Special Agent John Paxton. Paxton stood stiffly, arms at his sides, in jeans and a golf shirt, instead of the high-dollar suit and tie David was used to seeing him in. And he wore a frown that immediately made a knot appear in David's stomach, where there had been none just moments ago, before opening the door. Paxton nodded and said, "Hello David," but didn't extend his hand. The knot in David's stomach grew larger and clenched like a fist squeezing his insides till he felt queasy. Finally, David said, "Hello, Special Agent Paxton." David extended his hand, and Paxton shook it, but there was something undefinable and a little frightening even in that.

"Whadda' you want?" David said way more rudely than he intended. He felt cheated at being interrupted in his thinking. Then he asked, more civilly, "What's up. Did you get the guy? I haven't heard anything from you in a while, and I hoped no news was good news, like they say. So, you got good news?" David stood at the open door, in the boxers and Led Zeppelin t-shirt he slept in, waiting. The queasiness had grown into the awful beginning stages of nausea. He hoped that whatever Paxton had to say didn't make him upchuck on the agent's shoes. Paxton said, "David is there a place we can sit and talk?" There was a barely hidden hitch in his voice. "Yeah, I guess" David pushed the door open wider. Come on in," he said, and pointed toward the couch where he slept as often as not. Paxton walked to the couch, and eased down into it stiffly, all the way at one end. David dropped to the other end, as far away from as him as he could get.

They sat silently for a few moments, neither of them wanting to start a conversation, Paxton too hesitant, David too scared. "Finally, David said, insistently, "What is it?" Paxton took a deep breath. If they were playing poker and he had a 'tell' that would be a clear clue that he was about to say something bad. "Come on dammit", David insisted. "David, at five-o-five this morning a 911 dispatcher got a call from your mother. She was in an obvious state of distress." David didn't hear anything clearly past a call from your mother. He knew it had to do with Danny. The FBI didn't send out Special Agents to tell someone his mother's car had been stolen, or she was under arrest for speeding in a work zone. He was shaking so badly he could barely speak, Come on! Cut the cop double-speak! "Is it Danny?"

"I'm afraid so." Paxton's voice was shaky, too. "Your mother said she went in to check on Danny, because she hadn't heard him all night, and he usually didn't sleep thru without calling for a drink of water.

When Paxton used the word "didn't" instead of "doesn't", David fell apart. He started crying uncontrollably. In what was a decidedly un-Special Agent like move, Paxton put his arm around David's shoulders, and tried to stop his trembling. It was an exercise in futility. Finally, David looked at him through tear filled, but furious eyes and said, "What is it?" "Davey wasn't in his bed, Paxton answered. She panicked and went through the house looking for him." David instantly thought kidnapping. "Did she find him?" Paxton nodded. "She found him in the bathtub. He'd drowned." "What? How the hell did he drown in a bathtub? My mother wouldn't leave water in the tub. She's crazy-careful. She wouldn't leave water in the kitchen sink four feet off the floor, let alone the tub." "We're still trying to figure out what happened. Your mom was on the floor, curled up in a fetal position when the local cops got there. There was a cordless phone on the floor beside her." "Yeah; she's always been afraid of ending up on the floor, screaming, "Help, I've fallen and I can't get up! Was she hurt?" "Well," Paxton went on. "She wasn't able to talk to us yet. She had to be sedated."

David panicked all over again. First Patty, then Davey, and his mom, too? It was too much. He felt ready to explode. It must have shown on his face. "Was she hurt?" David shouted. "She's okay. She was in shock. They took her to the hospital as a precaution. She should be able to go home by tomorrow morning, if she wants." But physically she'll be fine." "What do you mean, if she wants?" "After what she's experienced, it might be better for her if she wasn't alone." "She won't be alone," David mumbled, almost too softly to be heard. "I know she won't," Paxton said quietly, and soothingly. He had questions that needed to be asked, but it was a touchy situation. Sadly, this was a scene he'd played and replayed way too many times in his career. Different, places. Different situations, But always the same scene. He knew the script, and through practice, he knew how to play it out; when to talk, when to pause and give the victim's family time to organize their thoughts and questions. To tell them to go at their own pace when he began asking questions, and be as accurate as possible. He waited a beat, to let David's fatherly defensive instinct mellow. He then said, "I'll probably have better luck questioning her away from the cr…" He let his voice trail off."

David shouted, "What were you going to say? The crime scene?" Paxton just looked at him. There wasn't anything else he could do.

"What in the hell happened? This wasn't an accident?" David fought to keep from screaming in the agent's face. Paxton shook his head. "The lock on the house's back door had been forced sometime during the night." David was too wrung out to think. He simply mumbled, "So?

The agent knew the meaning of the word from the past experiences he wished he'd never had. David wasn't expressing an uncaring "So what?" What he was doing was trying to figure what questions to ask, after the terrifying "So". Though Paxton knew it was his dreadful past experiences that made him able to do this part of the job, and do it well, he still cringed when he thought about how many family members he'd had to attempt to ease through this kind of experience.

Way back in junior-high school, a friend had said something that popped into his head at times like this; something that was so obvious, no one should be able to forget it even if he or she tried. He remembered the conversation verbatim. The guy was a neighbor five or six years older than he was. He made a living doing what too many people would look like a dream job. He had a small but nice garage behind his house. Inside the garage, he'd built a gorgeous dragster that he raced at least every other weekend, and won more often than not; making a decent living at it. One Saturday afternoon while under the car, with only his feet sticking out, like the Wicked-Witch of the West's feet stuck out from under Dorothy's house, he'd said to Paxton, "I hate doing this." "Doing what?" Paxton remembered asking. "Working on the car." "How can you hate it? It's an amazing car, and you race it all the time. I've seen your shelf full of trophies." "It's a necessary evil."

"What's that mean?"

"I don't like being a mechanic, but I love the race."

"Why do you love it so much?"

From under the car the guy had asked an obviously rhetorical question, "You ever drive a car that accelerates like a fighter jet?"

"No," he remembered answering."

"If you did, you'd understand."

The neighbor had stopped talking, feeling his explanation was sufficient. Paxton hadn't understood then, but did now; if the guy wanted to race, he had to work on the car. It was something he had to do to be a good racer; just like Paxton had to ease people through horrible times to be a good agent. It was his necessary evil. It was scary how often he had reason to remember that conversation. Now he forced his mind back to the present, and the job at hand.

"David, the crime scene guys are going over the house with a fine-toothed comb. I'm going back over when I leave here. I'm hoping your mom will be clear-headed enough to answer some questions by morning. You think you'll be okay? I can stay if you want."

David shook his head, a slow motion like a rusty machine struggling not to seize up. "I'll be okay. I learned all about this shit when Patty died." Paxton put his hand on David's shoulder; again, a very un-Special Agent gesture. "If I come back in a couple hours, you think we could talk a little, maybe see what we can come up with?" David nodded; the motion no smoother than the head shake had been.

"Maybe we can figure out who did it," Paxton said. David shrugged. "Knowing who the trucker was that killed Patty didn't bring her back." Paxton drew a blank. He shook David's hand. He did all the shaking. David just allowed his hand to be shaken. Paxton left, and headed to David's mother's house.

BROGAN

Wayne Brogan flopped from his stomach to his back, nearly rolling from the lumpy motel mattress to the grungy motel carpet. He managed to get a hand on the receiver of the braying phone. He sometimes missed the ring of old-fashioned phones. They were loud, but the sound didn't seem to drill into his head like the shrill screech that passed for a ringtone on modern phones. Before picking up the receiver, he glanced around the room. The irritating phone was the motels only concession to modern amenities. Even it was probably ten or twelve years old, but its gleaming black stood out like a shiny new dime in the concrete-block motel room, and it had the familiar four rows of three buttons. He wouldn't have been very surprised to find a rotary-dial model in the dump. The sheets and pillow cases were a gaudy orange color, probably picked up at a Howard Johnson's yard sale. The threadbare carpet was a green the color of faded limes. Where that comparison came to his mind from, he had no clue. Who really knew what the color of faded limes was. He'd never seen limes, or any fruit, fade to anything but brown, then black. He must have really gotten plastered last night, to be pondering over the color progression of rotting fruit. And, at that, a fruit that had no earthly purpose except to be squeezed down the neck of beer bottles of sunburned Mexican tourists, especially through his thundering headache. Whoever ran the place was either color-blind or just didn't care as long as things were cheap. Looking around the room, he figured it was the latter.

Wayne couldn't even remember the motel's name; Fancy Hill, or something like that, he thought. He'd been eighty percent tired, and ten percent drunk when he checked in, so that only left ten percent for things like memory. It didn't really matter. As long as he could remember where he'd parked his car, and the address in Las Vegas where he was going next, he was okay. Then he thought he recalled something from two days before, when he'd first gotten the call from the witch. In the bill pocket of his Harley Davidson wallet, tucked between a ten and a fifty was a piece of a restaurant placemat with an address on one side and a neatly printed list on the other. He marveled for a second at his own brilliance; both for remembering the information existed and for both remembering writing down the information and for remembering where he'd put it. Wayne wasn't stupid; just very focused. He felt it was one of his best traits.

He actually didn't care what the room was like. It had a bed and a commode to puke in if the hangover got the best of him. If he decided the name of the place mattered, he'd look out the window at the sign. It was where he'd been told to go, and when he got there this magnificent suite was reserved in his name, just like the witch said it would be.

When she'd first contacted him, and he still couldn't figure out how she'd found him, she'd only introduced herself as Donna, and the way she said it sounded shady. No stranger to doing very bad things for large amounts of money, Wayne was still surprised at what she wanted done, and what she was willing to pay to get it done.

Though she'd never said more than necessary to make her wants clear, she'd creeped him out, and Wayne wasn't prone to being creeped out easily. Even though she was a knock-out; no hooked nose or pointed hat, he'd immediately thought of her as the witch. It wasn't only what she wanted, but also the spooky, almost eerie vibe she put out.

When they'd sat across the table from each other in the restaurant, the first thing she'd done was tear off a piece of a placemat and written down the info about this crummy motel. Looking back, Wayne, never a deep thinker, gave thought to how confident she was that he'd do the job. Confident enough that she gave him the motel info even before she told him what she wanted, and how much it was worth to her. Then when she told him where he was to start, he couldn't keep a smile from spreading across his face. He didn't tell her, of course; he didn't want to lose the payday, but he'd have made the first stop on her list for free.

Wayne listened to what she had to say on the phone; actually, more of a question-and-answer period, to make sure he remembered where he was to go from here, he went to the bathroom, rinsed as much of the stale beer taste from his mouth as possible, took a piss and looked at himself in the mirror. He knew he was too identifiable, but it wasn't his fault. Or, at least not totally his fault. He wasn't a summer person, but when he was in the sun enough to darken his face the big curved scar over his left eye became too obvious to not be noticed. The scar wasn't his fault. But twenty-odd years before, on a drunken dare, he'd had the pentagrams tattooed on his eyelids. At the time he was thrilled with the way their stark blackness stood out on his naturally pasty complexion. And he was incredibly proud of the way he'd handled the pain. Then, the deeper he got into his wicked ways the more he realized how a man with pentagrams on his eyelids would stand out in a lineup. He ran water over his head and combed his fingers through his hair. He looked at his reflection again. The tattoos were all on him; he couldn't blame anyone there. The big scar was something altogether different. It stood out like a crescent moon in the night sky. Tattooed eyelids and the big scar made him as impossible to overlook as Jesse Jackson at a Klan meeting.

He never forgot who gave him the scar. The bone-deep gash had taken two days to stop bleeding, and then seeped through the gauze pads he taped over the wound for more than a week. It was several months before putting on a cap wasn't reason for brief but intense agony. A friend who worked as an assistant for a veterinarian told him the reason it took so long to stop bleeding was because his system had been loaded with not just alcohol, but also with Vicodin when he was clubbed on the head. It was not a clot-friendly cocktail. The same guy had stolen a lot of antibiotics for him. At one point he'd been taking twice the dose recommended for a Great-Dane. Wayne hadn't hesitated to take it. He wasn't afraid of any pill. But he was scared to death of the greenish look that the edges of the gash took on for a while. Lying on the cot in his buddy's apartment at night, he could swear he smelled the acerbic odor you smelled when you drove by the flattened corpse of some careless or simply unlucky animal on the road. When he'd asked his friend if he smelled it, the guy had answered with a firm no, but his nose wrinkled a little as he said it. Wayne resolved to ignore it, and for the most part didn't do too badly.

But through it all, he never forgot the big rock star who gave him the life-long headache. And all he'd been doing was what he'd done almost half a dozen times before. The chick was nothing special. So, what for him was a normal evening's recreation went south; Deep South, because of the hero rock star. He'd never seen the bastard come up on him with the bottle, but through every headache his mind's eye replayed the image of the guy on stage; screaming while the pentagram he wore swung like the pendulum of Satan's clock. The image of that pentagram taunted him every time the pentagrams on his eyelids stared back from a mirror.

Wayne was so stunned by his good fortune; the found money dropped in his lap, it blocked out all other thoughts. He never once paused to consider the odds that the hot but creepy woman would contact him, of all people, to do her dirty work. Even someone like him; whose mill-wheels ground continuously, but with remarkable slowness, couldn't have possibly believed it was pure coincidence. But all he saw was dollar signs; both then and now, as he left the lousy motel room on the next step in the fulfillment of the hand-shake contract that would make him a wealthy man. The dollar signs blocked out the memory of how that hand-shake made him feel dirty; not an easy accomplishment in a man of his stunted, under-developed character. He got in his Jeep and left Boise behind. As he watched the city shrink in his mirror he thought, 'What a stupid god dam place for a death-metal band'.

At the same time Wayne Brogan was slamming the motel room's door behind him, Agent Paxton was easing the back door of David's mother's house closed behind him. He stepped into an almost unbelievably clean kitchen. The front porch was cordoned off with multiple ribbons of yellow crime scene tape. A plain-clothes cop sat in an unmarked car across the street.

"Are you wearing gloves?" A voice came from the next room.

"What do you think?" Paxton said, irritated. "This isn't my first rodeo you know."

The owner of the voice from the other room must have picked up on Paxton's irritation.

"I know." The voice sounded hesitant and apologetic.

The man in the next room was Paxton's partner; George Alter. Alter was another street agent; one of the good guys who gets to deliver bad news. Though at sixty-one Alter was the oldest of the pair, but not by much, only six years, Paxton had been put in charge. It was like Danny Glover and Mel Gibson in reverse only not with such wildly different personalities. Despite his age, Alter had gotten approval of his request to attend a year-long school on forensic science. He'd fallen in love with it. And from what Paxton had both heard and seen he was very good at it.

"I'm in here, John. Watch where you walk! I haven't done a thorough scan of the floor yet. There might be footprints out there."

"Well, if there are, they ought to be easy to spot."

Paxton reached in an inside pocket of his jacket and took out two rubber booties and pulled them over his shoes. It always made him feel foolish to wear them, but they were necessary. He crouched, without touching the floor with his hands, and took a good look around the room. The floor looked as spotless from floor-level as it had when he was standing. "I'm coming in."

"Okay," Alter answered.

Paxton walked in a round-about path, staying away from the straight line from the back door to the room Alter was in. He didn't want to disturb any evidence the killer had left behind if he took a direct path. Alter was on his knees in a nicely appointed dining room. He was peering intently through a large magnifying glass at a small scuff mark near the bottom of the wooden trim around an archway on the far side of the room.

"What are you looking at Sherlock?" Paxton asked. Alter looked up at him. "Very funny, John. I'll have you know that this is standard operating procedure." "Maybe for Scotland Yard in eighteen-ninety. So, what did you find, constable?"

"So far, mostly just the obvious; the lock on the back door was forced; but you saw that when you came in. There were no clear footprints apparent in the kitchen or the hall that leads down to the little boy's room and the bathroom." Alter motioned over his shoulder with a nod. "What I'm looking at now, is a place where the paint has been knocked off this trim."

"That could have happened any time."

Alter looked up at Paxton, still looking through the magnifying glass. He had one eye squinted almost shut, looking for an instant like a near-sighted Cyclops. "Look around that kitchen, John. How long do you think a lady that keeps a kitchen like that could live with a big scuff like this?" He put his thumb over the mark to show its comparative size. "And, the wood in the mark is damp. I think our killer must have kicked it on his way out. He was hurrying and got careless. He must have gotten water splashed on him when he was holding the boy under the water. A scared two-year old would thrash around a lot. He was lucky the grandmother didn't hear. He was probably anxious to get gone."

"Anything else?"

"No prints yet, except the grandmother, and some really small ones down low on the TV screen and the refrigerator. I don't think there'll be any surprise who they belong to. And I think we can rule out robbery. There's a roll-top desk down the hall. It was locked. It doesn't appear to have been touched."

"How about the neighbors?"

"None of them were hit."

Paxton cleared his throat before answering. "So, he was targeted."

"The boy?" Alter asked. "Or maybe his father."

"The father?" Alter asked.

"Yeah, he has a history."

"A bad guy?"

"No. About six years ago, he was in the right place at the right time, and saved a girl from a wacko. They got married and it looked like a 'happily ever after' situation, then she was killed in a car wreck."

"Anything suspicious?"

Again, Paxton cleared his throat, clearly not enjoying relating the story. "No, it was just an accident. But I think we can rule out an accident here."

Alter spoke quietly, and sadly, "No, no accident here. I saw the little boy before they took him. There was a purple hand-shaped bruise that went halfway around his neck. Around the back of his neck. He was held face-down. Hell of a way for a little kid to die." Paxton shook his head. "Hell of a way for anyone to die. So tell me more about the scuff." He nodded toward the damaged door frame.

"Well," Alter said, happy the subject was changing. "The scrape is fairly high up." He paused and looked at Paxton's feet. "What do you wear, about a nine?"

"Nine and a half, why?"

"Well, by the height of the scuff, I'd say the guy was pretty big, and wears shoes about a size bigger than you." And I got a little scrap of his shoe leather."

"Enough to help?"

"Well, enough to know they're brown and regular cow hide. Nothing exotic; no alligator or snakeskin; nothing like that."

"Will that help us find him?" Paxton asked hopefully.

"No." Alter shook his head. "Sorry. but it will help tell us if we have the right guy when we find him."

"If he happens to be wearing the same shoes." Paxton sounded anything but hopeful.

"If we get somebody, we'll search wherever he lives. Unless he threw them away, we'll find them." Alter was trying hard to sound hopeful in the face of a nearly hopeless situation.

"Anything else?"

"No. The crime-scene guys didn't find any fingerprints or promising DNA sources in the rest of the house." He was already staring again at the scuff mark. "I'm going to take a swab of this, on the outside chance our very bad guy may have left epithelial behind. You can't put your shoes on and off, or tie them, without touching them. And touching leaves skin cells. I think the chances of it giving us anything are somewhere between nil and none. But trying anything is better than trying nothing. What are you going to do?" Paxton sighed tiredly. "Spend some meaningful time with my computer. I'll probably burn up the printer. I'll go over it all at home in the morning, with fresh eyes. By then Mrs. Boyd may be able to help us out. Call me if you find anything; anything at all. I'd love to give David Boyd some closure by putting a needle in this guy's arm. It won't bring his son back, but like you said; anything's better than nothing."

Talk about déjà vu all over again! Wayne Brogan was shocked awake by another shrieking telephone in another flea-bag motel with a name he couldn't recall, this one in Eureka, Nevada. It was where he'd stopped for the night after leaving Boise, after paying the rock star back for the crescent-shaped scar, and the years of headaches. The drive from Boise had taken seven-and-a-half hours with two stops for gas and put him four hundred and fifty miles from the kid he left floating in the bathtub. Again, he'd arrived at the motel almost too drunk to walk. Considering what his mission was, a drunk-driving bust didn't rank very high on his give-a-shit list. Again, the room was booked and waiting for him. It was no more luxurious than the last. The witch was paying him well. But whatever her end game was, she wasn't wasting any money on creature comforts on his behalf.

Not surprisingly, when he managed to grope the receiver from the phone, it was Donna the witch on the other end, checking up on him. Through the thundering headache; partially a leftover from the vodka bottle he'd taken to the skull years ago, but more from the twelve-pack of beer he'd consumed the previous night, he assured her he'd make his next appointment in Las Vegas that night. He'd managed the four hundred and fifty miles the day before, so the three and a quarter to Vegas should be a piece of cake. He had no personal stake in this stop, so he wasn't especially looking forward to it. Still, he was getting paid royally, even if he wasn't staying in a palace. The list she gave him when they'd first met wasn't very long, but she'd made it clear there was more where that came from if she chose to keep him traveling. He doubted he'd live long enough to spend all the money she was paying him. He'd given that little thought. The first stop had made it all worthwhile. From tonight on it was just a road-trip. What he was doing for the witch wasn't a far cry from what he'd done for the hell of it before; what he'd been doing in the hotel bathroom when the hero rock star interrupted. He figured anything he did from here on couldn't be a hell of a lot worse than what he'd already done. The things he'd done before the hotel bathroom were purely recreational. They were very bad, but nothing compared to drowning a two-year old. If there was a Hell, he no doubt had a confirmed reservation. Even that might not be too bad if he got to share eternity with the witch. She may be hideous inside, but she looked really good on the outside. It would be the ultimate case of making the best of a bad situation. But all that was in the future. For now, his sights were set firmly on Las Vegas. He may even treat himself to a real room there. He wondered if there even were any really crappy rooms in Vegas. She'd never said so, but he figured the witch had been booking him in the dumps to keep him out of the public eye. This time around he may bypass the place on her list. He had beaucoup cash left from the down payment she'd given him in the restaurant. The rooms were always paid for when he arrived. Other than gas, and a burger and beer here and there, he hadn't spent much. He wasn't being thrifty. Making money last a long time was an old habit. The ancient duffel bag he traveled with was heavy with the stack of bills, but he could definitely handle more. He'd be fine with the mission lasting five years, like the Starship Enterprise. He could almost hear William Shatner doing the voice-over in his throbbing head. Yes, tonight he would treat himself. But before he checked in, he'd find out what the phones sounded like. The thought of a nice room made him smile, but he wondered how the witch would respond. He knew she would find him, even if he didn't stay where she told him to. She would know where he was, of that he was certain. The first time he met her, it was like she was looking through him. It was part of that spooky, creepy vibe she put out. So it would be particularly important to do a very good job tonight. It was clear she wanted to keep him hidden, but she'd also made it clear she wanted his results to be as sensational, and as dramatic as possible.

Wayne showered with the hottest water the corroded shower head could produce. It was one of his quirks; most drunks took cold showers to sober up. But Wayne wasn't most drunks. He was a breed apart. He was a rare blending of psychopath and masochist, with alcoholism thrown in to make the mix more lethal. The psychopath in him made him appallingly ready to kill without hesitation. The masochist in him made him just as receptive to causing himself pain. He found a scalding shower distracting. It distracted him from the pounding in his head, and his overwhelming need for a drink. It was like the old joke about dropping an anvil on your foot to make you forget about a toothache. The hurt that came with steaming water pouring over him took his mind off of his other pain. The problem here was that the motel's water barely made it past warm. "Oh well", he thought. "Tonight would be different". After he finished his chore for the witch, he'd get a room with a hot tub, with the accent on hot. After the night's work, the hot water would do double duty; distracting him from his pounding head and getting rid of evidence. Blood could be very tough to wash off; especially if there was a lot of it. Wayne dried off after the lukewarm shower, got dressed and picked up the duffel bag. It was time to shake the dust of Eureka from his feet, and hit the trail. He got in his car; drove to a McDonald's and got a sandwich and coffee at the drive-thru. He made a last stop at a 7-11 for gas and beer, then pointed the Jeep south and headed for the bright lights of Vegas.

BELADONNA

Rain pounded on the skylight in the penthouse roof, even as the sun shone an unbelievably bright white. The kind of white you feel as much as see, when a laser spinning overhead at an out-of-control concert flashes you unexpectedly, and you slam the lids shut and hold them that way for minutes, afraid to try to open them; sure they'd be stuck shut, like they'd were welded closed forever. But this wasn't a pin point laser. This was just the incredibly broad expanse of white sky. She remembered being told by her grandmother, while she was still a child, that when the sun shone while it was raining it meant the Devil was beating his wife. It was one more thing she would remember to explore eventually.

Donna Grave rolled over to her back and stretched like a wakening cat. Her long- fingered hands curled into fists, each clutching a knotted handful of luxurious hand-woven silk sheets.

Rolling to her side, she let the stretched muscles in her long curvy legs, and extended arms and shoulders begin to relax. The new sense of calm looseness drew toward her center; progressing up her thighs to the area of her body where the moving senses paused to make itself appreciated, before moving on. The sense of uncoiling also was moving down past her head and neck, also pausing at her breasts for a moment, The moving sensations met in her belly, at a spot an inch above her navel. They met like the rails from the east and from the west met to form the continental railroad. There was no cheering or loud burst of fireworks; At least not outside her head. The practice was one she had adopted years before, after watching a seemingly sound asleep Siamese cat open its eyes, do a long slow stretch and release. The cat then instantly jumped straight upward and snatched an unlucky, low-flying finch from the air.

A glance at the clock showed her it was eleven a.m. Brogan should be at least a third of the way to Vegas by now. Donna looked around her bedroom. It really was her bedroom; not a motel room like the one she'd booked for Brogan. Sticking him in a series of shit-holes was one way to remind him who's the boss. She owned four houses; this one outside of Salt Lake City. Another sat on Long Island. Then there were the ones in L.A. and London. She truly was an international phenomenon. She'd spared no expense when choosing the houses or decorating them. Her profession had always been a lucrative one; and was becoming more so all the time. Like any business, all hers required was a good business model, and intelligence. Just like there were successful auto mechanics and ones that failed, it was all in the perception. The successful mechanics were the ones that made the cars purr along; at least till they were out of their shop. Or the dentist that convinced the patient that the secret to a life of painless bliss was the hundred thousand dollars' worth of veneers. At the same time some other dentist a mile away was putting a for sale sign in front of his office, and listing his chair and almost new 'mister thirsty' in trade magazines.

Donna was one of the prosperous ones; in fact, the most prosperous psychic in the world. All it had taken was a good business model and brains. Houdini wasn't the last ridiculously wealthy fool lining up to be fleeced; only the most famous. She was unique among the current pack that pass themselves off as mediums, in that she really did possess a formidable amount of true psychic ability. She hadn't become world famous by making furniture shake, or making rooms get cold for the amusement of the wealthy fool who wanted to contact his dead great-great uncle to see where his Confederate platoon buried the gold they stole when they raided the Union freight train north of Antietam. Or the wealthy woman in Tennessee who explained, in a voice made virtually unintelligible by a snoot full of vodka martinis, how desperately she desired to contact her dear departed poodle, Fifi, to find out who'd put the De-con in her steak tartar. She was sufficiently well known and well-connected to have a county sheriff and a city councilman join in at the séance. She said she'd always suspected the kid down the street; the one who stared at her with binoculars when she lay topless by her pool. But she didn't know the kid's name so when the scotch and the fervor of the séance got her wound up beyond control of her alcohol limited common sense, she began wailing, "You perverted bastard! You ogled me every goddamn day. Once you stared at me long enough, did you take my Fifi? What did you do to her before you poisoned her? I swear I'll have her dug up and get a vet to see if she was sexually assaulted. If I find out you raped my beautiful poodle, I'll kill you!"

When the old bitch got to the point of threatening lives, Donna had called the police. An investigation turned up that the woman had convinced herself her husband was having an affair, and had tried to punishing him by poisoning the dog herself. She'd then dismembered the poor animal and left the back quarter of the dog's body in her husband's bed. A wine bottle was inserted in the hideous mess she'd made of the dog's bodily orifices. The note found in the bottle said she hoped he enjoyed old Fifi, and that he'd managed to give the poodle the pleasure he hadn't gotten close to giving her for years. Near the end of the written ravings, the letters were pressed so forcibly into the paper there were torn ragged spots that made deciphering some words almost impossible. Enough was legible to recognize another very unpleasant threat. She promised on her mother's grave that when she caught the tramp he'd been running with, she'd make her parts look worse than the dogs did. Then she'd kill him.

The whole thing had been a damned mess. There was an investigation. The kid she'd accused didn't own binoculars, and would have needed x-ray vision to see her by her pool. Two houses and a garage stood between his window and her pool area. He was out of town at a high school ROTC training camp the entire time from when the dog went missing till after it was found poisoned. The husband had done nothing, and was, in fact, just a victim of a psychotic, drunken wife.

The woman begged to reach her murdered poodle, but had actually poisoned it herself and dismantled it like a victim in a canine slasher film, ended up in a state facility in a heavily padded room. The door of the room had a small slot in the wall down at the floor, so meals of finger foods that required no table-wear could be slid in on non-lethal foam plates. She wasn't committed because she killed the dog. She was committed because she threatened to slaughter damn near anybody, and everybody she could think of.

It was all over every newspaper and TV news show in the country, and even made world news. Bizarre things make good press; the more bizarre the better. What could have been the end for Donna was just the opposite. Suddenly all people could talk about was Donna Grave; the hero. She was the brilliant psychic who had helped the police put away a potentially homicidal psychopath. Who, with her phenomenal abilities, had contacted the other world and brought the truth to light. It had been the start of Donna Grave's one-woman empire.

The offering of valuable assistance to the police part of the story was pushed for all it was worth. It was pushed by both by Donna herself, and her new manager; Franklin Pace, who had no problem doubling as an ass kisser when needed. He made a hundred blitz pushes at radio stations, newspapers, and television stations, promoting himself as the one and only person who could produce perfect HD quality images of the entire incident. But the details of the event were always slightly fuzzy; the story left open-ended, the final chapter to be written at his convenience and supplied by his imagination. Of course, the Sheriff and city councilman in attendance were free to discuss the séance whenever they liked. Franklin Pace prescribed to the old adage; 'any publicity is good publicity.'

Despite his hounding, Donna refused to be interviewed by or to have her face plastered on supermarket tabloids. The resulting air of mystery only increased interest in her, so when she did do a TV or newspaper interview in the legitimate news field, it drew international attention. Her "60 Minutes" segment drew a higher number of viewers than the NBA finals. And as time passed, her fame grew. It had started as pure, dumb luck; the good fortune of having a deranged woman who wanted to reach her dead dog go off the rails and threaten to kill her husband, his imagined mistress, and anyone else whose name came to mind at that moment.

Donna's real psychic ability, which ran deeper than anyone believed, kept her in demand. In addition to a constant stream of private clients clamoring for her help in reaching their departed loved ones, she was contacted more and more frequently by police departments and the FBI for help solving tough cases. She consulted for Scotland Yard, and was instrumental in helping the New South Wales police in the capture of a serial killer in Sydney Australia. She made believers of the world-wide law enforcement community. She helped find a group of family hikers who were surprised by a sudden snow storm while in the Canadian North-West. She drew a map to their location exact enough that the RCMP sno-cat vehicles burst through the brush and into the hiker's make-shift camp just in time to have an offered coffee. All was well that ended well. The only disappointment was expressed by the eight-year-old boy. He was severely disappointed that they wouldn't be going back out on horseback. One more star on the 'Donna Grave Personal Walk of Fame'; that went the full hundred-foot length of the sidewalk that lay before her Los Angeles house. It was all because of the lucky fluke of having a well-heeled woman come out of the psycho-closet at just the right time. And as much as it grieved her to admit it, if she hadn't allowed Franklin Pace to convince her to let him hide a camera behind a curtain during the séance, she'd still be hustling the suckers P.T. Barnum made forever famous. So as Donna Grave nurtured and refined her cult of personality, Franklin Pace remained clueless of the extent of her true abilities and the extent of what she was planning, and of the part he would play in those plans.

BROGAN

Wayne Brogan rolled into Las Vegas at ten minutes till two. At a red light he took an instant to look at the address she had told him to look for. He figured to at least go by the place and check it out. If it was another of the dumps she'd been sending him to so far, he'd roll on by and find a nice place. Nice places must be a dime-a-dozen in Vegas. He might even get a room in a hotel/casino. One of the ones with the big shows; He wasn't interested in Wayne Newton or that Canadian chick; Céline something. But Siegfried and Roy; the two fags with the big cats might be pretty cool. On the drive-by he saw the motel the witch had set him up in was truly a dump; two story batten board with walls painted turquoise, festooned with black shadows of sea creatures.; a whale, an octopus, and the star of the wall mural; a huge sting ray, it's sheer size and otherworldly appearance undeniably formidable. The block wall surrounding the pool was no less decorated. Colossal starfish, several octopuses, a toothy barracuda, and another giant sting ray. No matter; He got a room in a major hotel, took a shower, got dressed, and over a surf and turf dinner, looked at the night's available entertainment fare. With a half dozen shots of single malt scotch to help him calm down and focus, he decided to pass on Rod Stewart, Katie Perry, and the Blue Man Group, but saw David Copperfield, and Earth Wind and Fire. As he left the concert venue, a glance at his watch showed he had no time to spare. He got his Jeep from the timed parking lot, went through a convenience store drive thru for a twelve pack of Bud, then topped off his tank and headed east toward the highbrow area that held his target. He drove toward the north side of the city, surprised at how rapidly civilization surrendered to a wasteland. He occasionally came on a pocket of large impressive homes clustered together between the largest dunes. His old jeep sometimes balked in protest of the sand that had drifted across the road in shallow dunes.

He plodded along through another hour of what felt like endless desert, but wasn't, only seemed like it because he was becoming anxious. The last thing he'd expected was to find himself looking forward to the violence and mayhem he'd signed on to do with the witch. Finally, in the middle of a long stretch of two-lane road totally devoid of landmarks, Wayne recognized his target. The house sat in a collection of similarly out-of-place homes. Its owner apparently was shooting for privacy, but missed the mark. In the cluster of homes, the one he wanted stuck out like the proverbial sore thumb. The walls and the turret that rose overhead were a glistening white. Either they'd been cut from pure white stone or painted snowy white. The roofs rose like a huge staircase. The white walls and the stepped copper roofs were accented by bright blue and green lights mounted on a spire atop the turret, always moving in lazy curves and arcs, like the searchlights in a prison guard tower. The lights also swept across a helipad visible on the roof. And to think it was a private home; not of royalty, but of a nationally known Death-metal star. Those bastards were popping up everywhere, like roaches when you turn on the kitchen light at three am. At least it made more sense; a death-metal band from Las Vegas (Sin City), than from Boise, Idaho. Idaho produced about twenty billion spuds a year; Clearly a front runner for 'Most Depressing State To Live In'. But it made absolutely no sense to him why the death-metal-mongers built a palace in the desert, like they craved privacy then lit the place up like Disneyland.

Wayne eased around the fortress of a house, looking for someplace inconspicuous to lay up for a while. The driving was slow but easy, the swirling winds spraying his windshield with fine powdery sand. The blowing sand made him feel more obscure to any guards or security cameras. Heat lightning flashed in the distance; first from one cloud to another, then from the bank of grimy clouds in the east to dunes hidden in the distance. The electric-light show left a clean ozone-charged odor behind. Wayne wasn't foolish enough to think the curtain of sand white sand was any kind of gift from God. If his goal had been to ransack the place, or even to break somebody's legs who had defaulted on a loan from the wrong people, he might have thought somebody big was cutting him a break. But based on his purpose for this visit, he didn't really think God had his back. He didn't truly believe in God, but either way, he was pretty sure he was on his own here; except for the witch, of course.

Wayne slowed till his engine was running at a slow idle. There was a gently curved driveway that circled the big house, its end blocked from sight behind the building. Wayne eased his Jeep to a spot behind the house, out of sight of the swinging lights that blanketed most of the property. The folded and refolded piece of paper the witch had given him on their first meeting was still in his wallet. He opened it and scanned it in the weak glow of the dome light. He found a pencil drawing of the layout of the house. There was something about that piece of paper that scared him. It was like a crazy book, a scary book with no end. Every time he unfolded it there was more of it, as if it was growing. The list of duties she expected him to perform was always there, expanding with each look. Sometimes it was a map to where he needed to be. Sometimes other information; like this floor plan. Everything he needed to know to fulfill the witch's plan, whatever it was. If Wayne had been smart enough to make the connection, he'd have realized he was simply a pawn in a gruesome game of chess. But that analogy was beyond him. He was like a wind-up toy. She aimed him in a certain direction and let him go, to do his worst. And since she'd found him, his worst kept getting worse. After sitting in the still Jeep for five minutes, watching for movement, he eased out the door and tip-toed to a big garage door. He punched in the code on the key pad by the door. The code was another of the bits of info the evil paper held. The door rolled up in almost total silence. A weak ceiling bulb came on, making it possible to navigate through the garage. Wayne's inner anger and envy neared the boiling point. He had to squeeze between a Ferrari and a Rolls to get to the door that opened into the house. He looked around the garage for something with sufficient heft to destroy the cars. But not seeing anything handy, he eased through the door and into a long hall with a Spanish marble floor. The witch hadn't said anything about needing a light, so of course he *didn't* need one.

How she knew the things she knew was something he'd never considered. The overspill of light from the swirling lights outside shone brightly thru the windows, casting a rainbow of colors ahead of him.

Wayne reached the long, curving flight of stairs shown on the magic map. Without putting his hand on the banister, he slowly climbed the stairs, stepping only on the end of each stair tread to avoid possible squeaky boards. That was something the witch didn't need to tell him. He'd climbed enough stairs in other people's homes in the middle of the night to be aware of the danger a loose nail holding a stair tread could cause. But by the third step he realized how unnecessary it was. The chance of him stepping on a squeaky board in this place was about the same as Obama stepping on a squeaky board in the white house on a midnight trip to the royal throne. At the head of the stairs, he turned left.

Lately it was almost as if he could hear the witch in his head. He didn't recall her map indicating he should turn left, yet there it was. The third door on his right was the door he wanted. He didn't know what was behind the door. "Monty, I'll take door number three." Whatever he found behind the door, he would deal with. The witch, who was an eleven on a scale of one to ten, would be in his head if he got stumped. He gave a brief thought to how somebody could look so good but feel so bad. Whenever such deep thoughts came to his mind, he shoved them behind the image of the pile of cash that was ever-present in his mind's eye. Thus hidden, the deep thoughts tended to stay away while he took care of business. He began whistling; something he never did anywhere, let alone in a house he'd invaded with very bad intent. It was irritating as hell; getting a song stuck in his head like a splinter you can't quite get out. So, now he whistled, 'Takin' Care of Business'. And he wondered what it would cost to get the guys from BTO to let them use the song for the soundtrack if they ever made a movie about him. Wayne slowly twisted the knob and went to see what was behind door number three.

BELADONNA

In Salt Lake City, Donna Grave glanced at the bedside clock and thought about her timeline and where Wayne Brogan should be at the moment. Though not carrying an overabundance of functioning gray matter, Brogan had turned out to be adequate, and at least so far, up to the task. Things seemed to be moving along nicely.

Tonight, would be the start of a pattern, and that's what she wanted; a pattern. It was something she'd picked up while consulting with law enforcement. In the mind of most rank-and-file cops, something happening once is an occurrence. Twice is a coincidence, though some good cops might pick up on it. Three times is a pattern. By the pattern stage, the world would notice. That's what she wanted; for the world to notice.

BROGAN

Wayne could have guessed a long time and would not have guessed what he'd find behind door number three. He stopped a step inside the door to reconnoiter the situation and decide how to proceed. He'd brought no weapons. He'd needed none to hold a two-year-old under water in a bathtub. Things were different here. He looked around the room and saw nothing that leapt to mind as the proper weapon. Still tip-toeing; he retraced his steps to the garage. He wasn't sure he needed to be quiet. There had been no indication anyone else was in the house. The star was probably tooling down the Vegas Strip in another million-dollar car. Just before opening the door connecting the kitchen to the garage, he paused to gaze down the length of the long hall that trailed off into the far reaches of the mansion. Way down the hall he saw a light from under a door. By now he'd been in the house for more than ten minutes; closer to fifteen if you included the time he spent in the garage in the process of breaking in. In that time, he'd heard no signs of movement. Other than the soft sound of his footsteps the house was completely silent. Well, it might be someone awake and reading. Or somebody trying to get a head start at sleeping off tomorrow's hangover. The light beneath the door flickered slightly, and Wayne pegged it as the glow of a TV. He eased through the door into the garage. The roll-up door he'd left open allowed enough moonlight in for him to look around more thoroughly this time. He'd paid no attention to the contents of the garage upon entering, excepting for the two million-dollar super cars he squeezed between. He hadn't noticed the pegboard-covered wall full of tools hanging neatly in carefully organized rows. Apparently, this star screamer was a mechanic. Or he had one service his fleet here in this garage. It only took a moment for him to spot the right tool for the job. Wayne put it in his back pocket and once more slipped quietly into the kitchen and down the hall to door number three. Under different circumstances the prize there would have made all this all worthwhile; even without the killing; as a bonus of course. He was making more money than he ever imagined for carrying out the witch's laundry list of mayhem. Wayne did the deed and exited the house. He pulled the house door closed; solidly but not hard enough to awaken anyone who may be holed up in the palace that death built. If someone was in the room with the light under the door, he or she never had a clue Wayne was anywhere near, let alone in the house. He was somewhat disappointed. This was becoming very enjoyable, and one more notch in his gun, so to speak, would have been all right with him.

As he drove away into the night Wayne wondered when his handywork would be discovered. He turned on the radio and tuned it to a news station. Nothing was mentioned by the time he got close to reaching his hotel. He parked his jeep up against the building, with the driver's window only inches from the curtains billowing in his room's window, blown by the hot dessert wind. He pulled a few CDs from his duffel bag, fed one into the jeep's radio, and cued up the song that seemed to suit the situation perfectly. After four or five beers, he flopped on the bed to get some rack time. He made a mental note to get a morning paper before he left town for the witch's next assignment. He was snoring in less than two minutes, satisfied with the way his life was going, and without a care in the world. In less than a moment, the dashboard radio was blasting out Bon Scott singing his ode to a Highway to Hell, loudly enough that the bass notes rattled the glass in the rusted old metal-framed window till it made a musicality all its own.

BELADONNA

Lying back in her top-of-the-line whirlpool tub in her master bath, Donna soaked her tight muscles, and tried to allow her mind to drift away on the man-made froth. Hot-pink colored heat light bulbs shone down on her; the hotness building within her as would the heat of a machine being driven to the bursting point, or an animal wound as tight as a spring, ready to strike, though she didn't know yet what the victim of the strike would be. The heat had a purifying effect on her, much as the sting of a steaming shower had on Wayne Brogan. She would have laughed had she known she had that in common with the slow-minded psychopath she'd enlisted to do her dirty work. She was confident her wide-ranging eye would tell her when Brogan had completed whatever horror he might perpetrate on her behalf; or in her name. She told him where to go and who to dispatch. The method was left up to his imagination. She was getting impatient; she couldn't wait to get the ball rolling. A flat-screened TV hung above the tub, its water-proof remote in easy reach. She had it tuned to the morning news. If her unique senses didn't tell her when Brogan had done his deed, the TV might.

As it turned out, the confirmation of an endeavor completed came from both sources within the space of a minute. As she sat in a tub full of bubbles, under the hot lights, enveloped in a sense of nirvana, a feeling came over her. Suddenly, nirvana was served up with a euphoria chaser. A feeling, almost indescribable in nature, filled her entire body. It was a wonderful feeling; though not quite as deep and satisfying as sex, it was every bit as enjoyable as a post-sex cigarette. Just a moment later, the TV screen was filled with images of dozens of pulsing blue and red lights clustered around a mansion set in the center of a desert. She knew Brogan had done his work. She would find out how later. For now, the TV and radio reporters were concerned only who would be the first to stick a microphone in the face of the grieving rock star and ask the inanest questions that could possibly come from the mouth of someone who was supposedly tasked with keeping the world informed; Something like, "How does this make you feel?"

Donna wasn't a sympathetic person by any stretch of the imagination, but she thought she might sick Brogan on the first reporter who asked such a ridiculous question. Just as punishment for being so amazingly stupid. At least some of the viewers sitting at home, gathered around the idiot box waiting for the juicy details would think the same thing; 'What a ludicrous question.' And if those enlightened few tuned in a different station the next time, the payback for asking the stupid question on the air might be unemployment. Reporting was a thinking person's vocation. She often wondered why it was called common sense, with it being so uncommon. Oh well, those were thoughts for another day. She turned the TV to a rerun of MASH she'd only seen a hundred times and slid down into the swirling water and dozed off, thinking happy thoughts.

PAXTON

Special Agent John Paxton sat in his kitchen, nursing his fifth cup of coffee. Sitting up till two am reading the same ten pages of information over and over took more out of him with each passing year; sometimes it felt more like each passing day. He certainly didn't have an eidetic memory, but could probably recite the police report word for word. He hadn't found Davey Boyd floating in his grandmother's bathtub. But he felt as if he had. He'd never shirked his duty since he'd been with the Bureau, but when the task of notifying David Boyd about his son's murder fell to him, he'd seriously considered clutching his chest and falling to the floor. An ambulance ride followed by an unnecessary physical didn't seem too bad. It was the reprimand, or maybe outright firing that would come after that, that he knew he couldn't handle. The Bureau was his life; it was what he lived for. And now he had a special purpose; a reason to live up to the word special on his cards and his badge. He _would_ find Davey Boyd's killer. All he hoped for was that he would meet the son of a bitch face to face, with no one else around to make him be rational, to calm him down. Or to keep him from doing anything he'd regret later.

He sat the empty fifth cup down and eyed the Mister Coffee on the counter, undecided whether a sixth cup would do him any better than the first five had. The question became moot. His cell phone rang in the bedroom, where he'd left it on the nightstand, next to his gun and badge. He got up and hurried toward the ringing phone, wishing he had time to stop by the bathroom and dispose of those five cups of coffee. He was almost jogging toward the bedroom and every step threatened to spring a leak he couldn't prevent. When he took the call, he wished he'd had the sixth cup, bladder be damned.

An hour later, Paxton entered FBI headquarters and headed for his office. His partner had beaten him in this morning. George Alter approached Paxton as he was preparing to open the door to his office. He held out a cup of coffee; not the swill from the coffee machine down the hall, but the good stuff from Starbucks. Paxton took the coffee and asked, "What's the occasion?" He opened the door and went in his office. Alter following him. Alter answered, "Nothing. I just know you, and I'd bet money you were up half the night going over the Boyd kid's murder."

Paxton nodded. "You'd win that bet." He took his jacket off and draped it over the back of a chair.

"Well, you look like hell."

"I feel like hell." Paxton took a spiral-bound note pad from his back pocket.

"Sit down."

Alter took a chair. "What's up?"

Paxton flipped a few pages into the pad, and said, "I got a call this morning from the Las Vegas office."

"About what?"

"They got something that might be related to the Boyd case."

Alter leaned forward, anxiously.

"This morning the 911 operator took a call from a man that reported a murder."

"What's that have to do with the Boyd case?"

Paxton again looked at the pad. "The call took them to a Mansion out in the desert, five miles from the city. They found a dead girl."

"Yeah?"

"Yeah. The house belongs to a Gordon Tate. Gordon Tate is the singer for a death-metal band '**Crucifixion.**' He uses the stage name Judas."

George Alter's wind was up at the mention of death-metal. "So, who was the victim?" Paxton glanced quickly at the pad.

"Her name was Sandy Tate. She was Gordon Tate's fifteen-year-old sister. She apparently stayed there most of the time. She was sleeping off the Champaign she was too young to be drinking at one of her brother's parties. He's apparently a real party animal."

"What a shock." "Well," Paxton continued, "While big brother was entertaining a friend in a bedroom fifty feet away, someone broke in and offed little sister. He didn't hear a thing. He was probably in worse shape than his sister.

"How was she killed?" Alter asked, not because he really wanted to hear all the details about a dead fifteen-year-old, but because it was his job. Paxton took a deep breath. "Somebody put all eight inches of an eight-inch Philips screwdriver in her left ear."

Alter looked at the ceiling. "Jesus."

"Yeah… Jesus."

George Alter sighed, and Paxton thought it was the saddest sound he'd ever heard. Then Alter said, "Death by drowning and death by screwdriver; that's pretty different methodology. You think it could be a different guy?"

"Anything's possible, but Boise and Vegas are only a dozen hours apart by road, and only three hours by air. What do you think the chances are that family members of two death-metal singers are murdered by two different perpetrators within a couple days of each other strictly by coincidence?"

Alter snickered quietly, but there was absolutely no humor in the sound, only irony. "Until a couple days ago, I didn't know there were two death-metal singers." Paxton said, "I think it's more likely it's the same guy, who for whatever reason is fixated on death-metal singers, and his methods are strictly based on convenience and opportunity. In the Boyd case, he came in the back door and passed the bathroom on his way to the boy's room, so the he knew where the bathtub was, and it was convenient.

The intruder at the Tate mansion came in through the garage, and according to the agent I talked to, that garage had more tools in it than the hardware department at Sears." Alter said, "John, pretty much all I know about death-metal is what I've read on the internet in the last two days. Do you think it might be some vigilante? Maybe some overzealous religious fanatic who thinks it's his mission to save the world by killing off the loved ones of musicians who scream off key and play out of tune?"

"I thought you didn't know anything about death-metal?"

Alter said, "Only what I found on YouTube. What do you think?" "I think I should check for recent assaults or threats on death-metal musicians. I imagine these guys get a lot of hate mail from pissed-off parents worried for their kids. We'll have to weed out the everyday stuff from anything serious, Alter said. "That shouldn't be too hard. These bands probably travel with security, even more than other bands, just because of the product they're promoting. Those would be the people to talk to; Security. They should know from experience how to tell the everyday bullshit from the kind of stuff a psycho like this would say. And hopefully if they did get anything really sick, they turned it over to the local police. If they did, they'll have run it for prints, and a lab work-up. If they'd found anything, we'd have already heard about it. If they didn't, we'll have our lab go over it, just in case." Alter gave a discouraged sigh. "So, what do we do now, just wait for another one?" Paxton picked up his jacket, shrugged into it, and said, "The Vegas report is on your computer by now. I want you to go through it and look for similarities to the Davey Boyd case. You've got a better eye for the small stuff than I do."

"And you?" "I'm going to Vegas. Whatever I find there I'll send to your phone." "If there were never any threats made hideous enough for the band's security people to turn over to the police, I'll have a sit-down with them and see if I can help them recall anything they might have forgotten or overlooked." He took a last gulp of the coffee Alter had brought and dropped the cup in the waste can next to his desk.

When it hit the bottom of the can, a dozen or so drops of coffee jumped over the lip of the can and hit the carpet. He shrugged. "The cleaning crew won't like that." Alter said, "Life's rough. It won't be the worst thing they'll ever have happen to them." "Yeah," Paxton said. "I imagine everyone on the crew will live his or her whole life without having a screwdriver jammed in an ear." He picked up his brief case and left the office. Fifteen minutes later he felt the muted thump of landing gear folding into the belly of the FBI's Gulfstream jet. And he watched the farmland below seem to pitch as the plane silently banked in an easterly direction toward Las Vegas.

BELADONNA

Donna sat on the floor of the east-facing sunroom of her house, her legs folded beneath her and her head down till her chin almost rested on her absolutely perfect chest. She'd always thought her boobs were one of her best features, second only to her hair. Short cropped, and black as the deepest corner of a coal mine; it framed her face like a pitch-black wreath. One thing Franklin Pace had stressed ever since he became her manager was that being beautiful was a huge plus for someone who strove to be in the public eye as much as possible. Virtually everybody had preconceived expectations about a psychic. To many, the word psychic conjures images of a dried-up old hag with a scarf around her head, sitting at an ancient wooden table in a dark room staring into a crystal ball. When they turn on the TV and see her lounging on a towel by the ocean, and realize that she has the best bikini body on the beach, it's like plastering the image on the inside of their eyelids. It's like seeing a singer who you would have bet from his voice would look like Meatloaf and seeing Tom Petty. It's the first thing you'll tell your friends about when you see them; "Hey, did you see that psychic, Donna Grave on the news last night? She's nothing like I pictured. Damn, she's hot!" The result was especially effective on horny old men and lesbians. Pace was pushing her to do a calendar; twelve images of her sitting gazing at a cloudless sky or staring into a fireplace, etc., depending on the season. She would always look angelic and wrapped up in thoughts that could only benefit someone. Always, of course, wearing little enough clothing to make the calendar a must- have in every garage and truck stop.

But now sitting on the floor, in a meditative state, she was thinking about where to go on the next step on her quest. That was what she considered it to be. It wasn't just a murder spree concocted on a whim. She had very definite goals. Goals that when achieved would change everything. And as she studied the situation carefully, she was glad Franklin Pace had come to mind. She may just have an important role for him to play in this rapidly unwinding drama.

But for the moment, she turned her mind back to Wayne Brogan. He'd done well for her. Of course, he was no more than a puppet. The longer she pulled his strings, the easier it became. Now, all she had to do was to think about she wanted him to do and it was as good as done. The list she'd given him in the beginning was just a jump-start. As she'd expected, he was the perfect man for the job. She'd had a feeling about him, and her feelings were never wrong.

He'd turned out to be the perfect wind-up toy; she wound him up and let him go. He'd keep going till he wound down or something got in his way and stopped him. With her in his head rewinding him he would never stop moving forward. If something or somebody got in his way he would handle it, by whatever means necessary. But something beyond even her expectations had occurred. With her in his head he'd become a windup toy that gathered speed instead of slowing down. Even in her initial list, she'd only told him the "where" and the 'who'. The how had been left totally up to him. He was told only to make it spectacular, something that would take the media by storm. Thus far he'd performed spectacularly. Finding a way to top a two-year old drowned in his grandmother's bathroom was a tough one. As it turned out, a screwdriver in the ear of a drunk fifteen-year-old had done the trick. It helped that Tate was more well-known than Boyd. A celebrity naturally gets the press. It only makes sense. But it was Boyd that mattered. He was the lynch-pin of her endeavors. He was the one that would make her the focus of every eye in the world. At least till it was too late. David Boyd and his little boy were special to no one on the planet except her; and maybe the grandmother who'd found poor Davey floating like an out of place pool toy. How she knew The Boyd boys, father and son, were the first step in a journey of countless miles was simple; she just had a feeling. And she never questioned her feelings. One more task for Brogan and she would have to decide what to do with him. He was the textbook psychopath. And she had taken advantage of his nature; it was one of her special talents. She needed someone not just crazy, but very crazy. And it was easier to make a crazy person crazier than to make a sane person crazy. And Brogan's crazy knob went to eleven; just like Spinal Taps amp. With a little more pushing, she might even add a twelve to his crazy knob. Donna picked up the phone and called Franklin Pace.

PACE

When Franklin pace's phone rang, he checked caller ID before answering. When the phone rang on his personal number, he knew the list of possible callers was limited. He only gave that number to the clients he knew could make him the most money. Or the ones whose pants he wanted to get into. Or in the case of Donna Grave, both. As long as he'd been in the agent business, he'd nurtured the public belief that he was gay. It seemed to be a plus in his occupation. He knew Donna saw through his charade. He also knew she didn't care. Since the day they'd met he knew Donna Grave *always* had her own hidden agenda. And he was sure her agenda didn't involve allowing him into her pants. Staring at the phone before hitting answer, he thought for just an instant that he'd die to know what that agenda was, then after just as brief of an instant, wished very hard that he'd never had that thought.

Pace answered, "Morning, Donna. How's my favorite client doing today?" There was a moment of silence. A chill raced up Pace's spine.

"Franklin, get packed."

"Well, Donna. Loquacious as always, I see. Where am I going?"

"Fresno." Pace was annoyed at being treated like her lackey, but wasn't just hesitant to respond angrily; afraid to. He mustered all the self-control he could manage, and spoke evenly, "Why am I going to Fresno?"

"Does it matter?"

The chill retraced its path up his spine. "I don't suppose it does. And when am I going?"

"Take time for a nice lunch," she said graciously. "Leave by one p.m. Enjoy a leisurely drive. Put the top down, and enjoy the weather. Southern California is such a beautiful area. As long as you're there and checked into a nice hotel by nightfall, that will be fine. Just get a receipt, and I'll reimburse you. Some motels give a discount if you pay with a credit card. You should think about that. I'm not made of money, you know."

There was that speedy chill again. "Donna, I don't have a convertible."

"Go rent one, from a company that has an office in Fresno where you can drop it off."

"Drop it off?" Pace was rapidly becoming very worried.

"Yes," Donna replied sweetly. "You'll be staying for a while." "How long of a while? And what will I be doing in Fresno?" "Franklin," she answered, again in that unsettling, syrupy voice. "I feel that in the time we've been associated, we've become close. Very close. I know that I often feel like I know what you're thinking. And I hope you feel the same about me." Her voice had grown husky, almost a deep purr. "I'm sure if you think about me; think very hard about me on the drive, it will come to you. You'll know what to do when you get there."

Franklin Pace made the drive that typically took over twelve hours in less than eight. Donna said to be in Fresno by nightfall, and he intended to make her happy. Aside from his dream of getting her in the sack, he found that there was something a little unnerving about her. Creepy was far too strong of a word, and he never thought of her as 'the witch' as Wayne Brogan did. But she occasionally made him feel a little frightened. The longer he was acquainted with her, the more he recognized that the abilities he'd hired on to promote were real. Sadly, for Franklin Pace, he didn't appreciate just how real, or how far-reaching.

BROGAN

Wayne awoke in a beautiful room. It was like a totally different world from the series of crappy holes he'd been waking up in since embarking on the witch's national murder tour. Again, he'd found a reserved room awaiting him when he arrived. The list was lying on the bedside stand. He blinked several times to clear the sleep from his eyes. He was only able to clear his vision to a point. He could blink away the sleep, but not the lingering effect of the previous night's scotch. The beautiful hotel had an equally beautiful bar, where he'd stayed till they place closed up at two am. Squinting, he peered intently at the list; the one written on a piece of a diner placemat. He'd come to realize the list was no longer necessary. There were only two destinations designated; the ones he'd already visited. The first was where he'd held the kid's head under water, the second where he'd given the cute little blond with the streak of blue in her hair a pierced brain to match her pierced nose. After that one, a horrible sense of disappointment had enveloped him. He was sorry the list ended. He was no longer doing her bidding just for the money, though he'd definitely not flushed the remaining twenty or thirty thousand down the toilet. He'd blown every bit that much in Vegas, where he'd treated himself to the wonderful room he so desired. The down-side was the casino on the hotel's first floor. The generous management saw to it he was never wanting for liquid refreshment as he stood at the one-armed bandit, continuously pulling the lever like he was also a machine. The twenty thousand had gone away fast. He'd hardly noticed. There were horns sounding and lights flashing every minute, to announce another winner somewhere in the huge room around him. He, almost as frequently, heard the loud ringing of a cascade of coins gushing from a machine somewhere to his right or left way down the seemingly endless row of slot machines. No coins gushed from the machine he'd stood in front of for hours. But the liquor was free, and the place was crawling with hot women; each of which was wearing less than the one before. It was like a competition, and he was the winner. He was experiencing things he'd never imagined. The high point of his previous gambling experiences was turning a full house in a dive bar with hookers milling around the room; each one looking sleazier than the one before.

Now, lying on the plush pillow-top mattress in the beautiful hotel room, he decided that the witch had sent him here for his own good; if he'd stayed in Vegas he'd have ended up as broke as he was before he met her.

The major thing that baffled him was that though the list ended after two stops, here he was. Once he'd gotten in his Jeep the morning after killing the girl with the screwdriver, it had come to him. He knew where to go, and who to dispatch.

She'd spoken in his head. He was so glad she had. On this trip, he'd found his proper calling. He'd discovered how truly resourceful he was. The where and the who came from her, but the how was left up to him. He thought of the years he'd squandered a skill he wasn't even aware he possessed.

Looking out the window, he wondered what was next. Though this stop wasn't on the list, he had no doubt the witch would direct him. For the first time, he felt a pang of guilt for thinking of her as the witch. The feeling didn't last. Looking out at the skyline, with a gorgeous backdrop of a vibrant multi-colored sunrise, he decided he would probably like Fresno.

DAVID

For the first time since Special Agent Paxton had knocked on the door to tell him his mother had found Davey floating in her bathtub, David looked at the guitar hanging on the wall. It was as black as his mood had been lately. The guitar was specially made, and had been a large cash outlay for him in the pre-recording contract days. The advance he'd gotten before Patty's death, the one he'd used to buy the engagement ring she'd never known about, was just the beginning. During the period when he was barely able to drag himself out of bed before noon, the rest of the band went in the studio and laid down their tracks. He was okay with it. They couldn't be expected to stop living just because he had. Once he'd gotten to the point where he was able to function, he added the lead guitar and vocals.

The album had outperformed all expectations. Only a week before somebody murdered Danny, the contract was signed for two more albums. The rest of the band had already started cutting the follow-up album, using another guitarist and vocalist. Again, David was okay with it. He even recommended the guys who replaced him. The trade papers made a big deal about it taking two people to take his place. It was the first time since Joe Walsh left 'The James Gang". The rest of the guys in the band made it clear that he was welcome back when he was ready. Then Special Agent Paxton knocked.

And the checks kept coming in. He was becoming independently wealthy for doing nothing. But they were recording songs he wrote, and the royalties were huge. There was even talk about a Grammy: something that never happened to a death-metal band before.

BROGAN

Wayne spent the whole day waiting and listening. He was waiting and listening for Donna Grave to talk to him. Without realizing it was happening, he had gone from being her employee to being her puppet. She had opened his eyes. He knew that when he heard from her it wouldn't be by telephone, it would be in his head. He waited for her voice in his head like a dog will wait for its master to say roll over, or play dead. She had trained him like the owner trains the dog. She'd given him treats to do her bidding; first a boatload of money, then a lavish trip to Las Vegas, and along the way, the best treat of all; a chance to be his own boss. He was like a sub-contractor. He was just like an electrician. Like an electrician, he knew where he had to be, and when he had to be there. But the electrical sub-contractor decided what wires to twist together. Wayne was the murder sub-contractor. He made the decisions what wires to twist. He decided how long to hold the kid underwater. And he decided what screwdriver to bury in the drunk chick's brain. He remembered how he'd wondered just before he did it if blood would splash on the blue streak in her hair. It hadn't, but it made a fan-shaped pattern on the sheet. He'd thought at the time that it would be a cool decoration if it were painted on the hood of his jeep.

But now, he was well beyond the training stage. Now he was like the dog that would do whatever his master said, even without having a Milk Bone dangled in front of its nose. He'd drunk the Kool-Aid. She had him by the balls, and wasn't likely to let go. Room service brought him a filet and six Heinekens for lunch. When he was done eating, he flopped on the bed for a nap. He hoped she would talk to him while he slept. He was getting impatient.

He wasn't disappointed. He woke up just after five p.m. The first thing he saw was the ornate-looking chandelier dangling above him like a UFO against a bone-white sky. A glance around reminded him where he was. The room-service tray sat on the floor a dozen feet from the bed. He belched, and tasted beer-soaked steak. He searched his mind and was delighted to find that his wish had been granted; the now familiar sultry voice had spoken to him while he slept. He now knew where to go, and who he was to visit her horror upon. The sun was on the other side of the building from his window, but he could tell by looking at the fuzzy-edged shadows across the street that it was coming on evening.

A sense of urgency filled his head. He went to the bathroom and ran water over his head under the sink faucet. The action brought to mind the frequent evening's entertainment he used to enjoy in what seemed like another life. Back then he'd considered rape as innocent recreation. If battery was necessary to ease the process, so be it. But all that had changed the night the rock star blind-sided him with a bottle. Then came the headaches, and the liquid diet; usually acquired at a liquor store. His life had become pure misery after that night. All because he was holding some bitch's head under running water. It wasn't any worse than the water-boarding the CIA used at Guantanamo Bay. If it was good enough for the U. S. of A. it was good enough for him. Wayne Brogan was nothing, if not patriotic.

Well, it had taken years, and a push from a scary woman with a great ass, but he'd gotten back at the rock star. Was it the Bible that talked about a pound of flesh? He wasn't sure. But he figured the kid that couldn't breathe water weighed about twenty-five pounds. So he'd gotten twenty-five times his pound of flesh. And it had only been the beginning. Since then, he'd punished another rock star. The tally so far was two and counting. After he awoke from his nap, he knew who and where his next kill would be. He could hardly wait till night. But he was more cautious than crazy. Even though he wasn't coherent enough to recognize the fact, even that bit of common sense was planted in his mind, courteously of influences of which he couldn't conceive. Influences that not so long ago he thought were the things of late-night movies, hosted by someone with pale pancake makeup, dressed as a vampire or some other fictional creature that looked as real as the Wicked Witch of The West's flying monkeys. Though now he wasn't so sure he'd dismiss flying monkeys as pure fiction. He'd done many bad things in his life, including rape and murder. Things most people would consider more than bad; evil. But now he had no delusions about what he was. He was evil. Drowning a child and piercing the brain of a teenager surely qualified him for the title. And he'd done those things with no compunction; in fact, looking back he found only satisfaction; the satisfaction that came with a job well done. And tonight would be one more feather in his cap. He wanted desperately to satisfy her so she'd keep going. He still had no idea what drove her, but he knew what drove himself; and that was enough. He watched anxiously for the sun to drop below the horizon.

When the last jagged shadows of the Fresno skyline faded across the street a dozen floors below the window of his room, looking like a smile missing some teeth, he got ready. He changed into a combination of red sweat pants and a San Francisco 49ers jersey.

The clothes were the perfect color to hide blood. There was always the chance he might get stopped for crossing the center line or weaving on the trip back from his mission. He always did a lot of weaving when he drove; because he was most always drunk or getting over being drunk, or attempting to.

He rode the elevator to the lobby, and hurriedly left the hotel. He didn't want to be late for a very important date. The valet brought the Jeep to where he waited, and wrinkled his nose as he got out. The smell from the burger wrappers and crushed beer cans littering the back floor had gotten to him. He gave Wayne his keys and said thanks. He let go of the keys as soon as possible, anxious to be out of Wayne's vicinity and not wanting to delay his exit. The valet had seen something unnerving in Wayne's eyes. Wayne paused at the stop sign at the parking lot exit, and tried to clear his mind. Then her mind spoke to his. He turned right into the heavy traffic flow; the good people of Fresno heading home from work, wondering what would be good for dinner. Wayne felt sure their evenings wouldn't be as interesting, or as satisfying as his.

He arrived at his destination and parked a block away from the house at what he hoped was a discreet distance. A disappointed NASCAR driver once said in an interview after coming in second in a big race; "Second place is the first loser." Well so far this guy was the first loser. After offing the kid at grandma's house, he'd driven past the rock star's house, just out of curiosity, to see how the other half lives. He'd been surprised. The place was unremarkable; a plain vanilla cube in a lengthy row of plain vanilla cubes. In the brief glance he got as he circled the cull de sac, he saw the grass needed cut, and from the street it looked as though the windows were dirty. Then he'd visited the mansion in the desert.

Now he watched the house closely, like a cop on a stake-out. In the limited experience he'd had with the homes of the rich and famous, this guy was the first loser. The house was typical southern California; strong Mexican influence, tile roof and stucco walls. There were no spotlights and no helipad, but his grass was trimmed and as best as Wayne could see in the fading evening light, the windows looked clean. The sky was leaden; the clouds thick but distant, and moving away. The sky was clearing as they departed. He waited. Soon the conditions would be perfect for his requirements; full dark, no stars.

Wayne didn't delay long. His patience was wearing thin. There were many things he could rush, but the onset of night was beyond his control. Finally, when he could wait no longer, he slowly swung the door of the Jeep open. The hinges creaked. The sound was very small, but to Wayne seemed deafening in the dead still night. When he stood beside the Jeep he became very still, his head swiveling, as he scanned the area from horizon to horizon. Nothing moved, and not a sound came to him from the silence. He took a deep breath and walked toward the house. He approached the front of the house, crossing the lawn from the street toward the front porch. His sureness, bolstered by his success at his first kills, made him bold. But in his head, she had told him this time would be different. His Hubris-fueled arrogance had gotten him this far without hesitation, but he didn't feel that going in the front door would be prudent. Instead, he crept to the side of the house and started circling the structure with his ear against the wall, listening for activity within.

If someone could have seen him in the darkness, he would have looked like a man easing his way along a ledge high on a skyscraper. When he turned the corner to the back of the house, the south-facing side, that most often faced the sun, he moved even more slowly, in case the designer of the building had included more windows there to take advantage of the fact. With his chest to the wall and his ear pressed against the stucco, he eased along. In his head, he heard the witch's voice. She spoke in a whisper; her voice mell; and at the same time authoritative, in charge. Her message was simple, he was to be careful. This one was different. He would have liked to think she was worried about his well-being, but he knew better. She cared only about his success. Finally, his left hand encountered something other than the course pebbly stucco. Exploring with his fingers, he found a vertical bar of metal; three or four inches wide; cool to the touch in the warm night. He thought how easily he could have missed it and discovered what was beyond it noisily instead of silently. His mission could have ended in failure right here. He kept inching along, even more slowly and cautiously than before. Beyond the metal bar, his hand found a wide expanse of glass. He moved on, careful not to press too heavily against the glass, for fear of rattling it or possibly breaking it. If that happened, all hope of a surprise attack would go right in the shitter.

At last, his fingers encountered another vertical metal bar, followed by more glass. Wayne understood he had found a sliding double-door. He grasped the center bar and pulled gently, not knowing if he was pulling in the right direction or not. The door moved. This rock star was apparently the careless type, who didn't feel the need to lock his doors. He probably wouldn't continue drawing breath long enough to regret his carelessness. Wayne's heart leapt at his good fortune; just a small leap. Just a gentle push and the door slid easily and silently for a foot or more, and then jammed on something stuck in the bottom track; probably a pebble or chunk of sun-hardened sand. Wayne pulled harder. Finally, the door did slide; but this time it wasn't silent. The door jerked a good half-foot in a single lurch, making a loud scraping sound. Instantly, a light came on in the room. Inside the glass door was an opaque curtain almost the full width of the glass. Wayne squinted to see past the edge of the curtain, but could see only a bright, unidentifiable source of the light in the otherwise total darkness. He heard movement beyond the glass. Suddenly he saw movement. A shape was moving rapidly toward him; backlit by the light; a big shape.

Wayne's nose was pressed against the glass. For the first time since he'd taken on the witch's rein of mayhem, he felt fear. It hit him like a punch to the gut. He almost turned and ran off into the darkness, but she would know: of that he was certain, and of that he was afraid. Fear of her won out. Wayne stood frozen, his face against the glass, uncertain what to do. Then, the decision was made for him. The filmy drape was torn away, and the door he still held onto was thrown open. He tried to hold onto it, to stop its movement, but couldn't. The metal frame of the door was torn from his hand, folding back several of the nails on that hand. The pain and the shockingly rapid flow of blood pouring over his palm were barely noticed. Before the sliding door even came to a stop, a huge hand had ahold of his collar, and he was yanked through the door. His toes caught the bottom of the door's track, and he pitched helplessly forward off his feet. But he didn't fall to the floor. Now the hand that pulled him in also held him up. Before he could look around, the person who held him started shaking him. Wayne let out a helpless yelp. Whoever shook him was remarkably strong. Wayne flopped around helplessly, the motion snapping his head back and forth. A terrible pain shot through his neck, so sudden and severe he screamed. Not a pitiful yelp this time, a full blown, balls-to-the-wall scream. He pictured himself dropping to the floor, helpless; paralyzed, when, or if the monster who was shaking him ever let go. Fortunately for Wayne, a distant car horn blared in the street for some unknown reason. Later he wondered if the witch had done it. She could think in his head, but could she control things? The hand shaking him let go, and he dropped face-down on the floor. Then a bare foot hit him in the side. He was fortunate the foot was bare, or most of the ribs on that side would have snapped like twigs.

As Wayne rolled helplessly around on amazingly soft carpet, he finally got a look up at the man who'd nearly killed him in a matter of seconds. The man was huge. Not fat huge, Lou Ferrigno huge. Wayne lay there transfixed. The man wore only boxer shorts. His legs looked like tree trunks and the light from the bedside lamp reflected from the sweat on his rippling muscles. The huge man lifted his foot and Wayne cringed and shrunk back, as much as possible, wrapping his arms around his head. He realized he was whimpering like a kicked puppy. Then the man's huge foot came down on his left hand. He heard his own bones snap, and the pain was huge, by far worse than anything he'd ever felt. And he had been in his share of fights before. The pain of having his eyelids tattooed paled by comparison. He stupidly thought as he writhed on the floor, it could be worse, at least I'm right-handed. My trigger finger will still work. Before the huge man could pull his foot back, Wayne thrust his head out and bit down on his big toe. The man shook his leg furiously, trying to pull loose, but Wayne hung on, biting down as hard as possible, knowing that letting go would be suicide. He shook his head like a terrier shaking a rat. In a moment, blood gushed into his mouth, and the big man's toe tore off. Wayne turned his head and wretched, spitting the toe out to keep from swallowing it. The giant stepped down on the injured foot, lost his balance, and went down. Wayne lay on the floor, a solid mass of head-to- toe pain. He thought of the witch, wondered if she knew she was sending him to murder the Incredible Hulk. At that moment, he could cheerfully kill her for doing this to him.

Then she spoke in his head, and he forgot everything else, His desire to kill her, the anguish of his shattered hand, everything but her voice, clear as a bell, "Get up Wayne. You're not finished yet; you have a mission to accomplish. You don't want to disappoint me, do you? I don't like being disappointed. I can be very nice, and I can do nice things for you, if you don't disappoint me."

He saw her in his mind's eye, and she looked like the most beautiful thing he'd ever seen. Her eyes looked at him, the sultry green of a cat's eyes. By that point, Wayne was beyond rational thought, so he wasn't aware he was smiling. Then she said; "But if you disappoint me, I can be not so nice. I can be very not-nice." In his confused mind's eye, she changed. She was still beautiful, but frightening. The black hair; that normally ringed her face, was stirring, as though moved by a brisk wind blowing from behind her. Strands of it blew across her face in a way Wayne would normally have found sexy. But her eyes, no longer cats-eye green, made her not sexy, but terrifying. It was as if they had sunken, till they were staring out from dark shallow pits. They were so heavily ringed with black; it looked as though they were peering out from a gloomy abyss. But within the dark circles shone eyes that made his blood freeze. They were as red as a fire engine, and blazed from within with the unmistakable fire of a furnace. Looking into them was like peering through the twin lenses of binoculars focused on Hell. He knew she was only in his head and was still frightened beyond anything he ever thought he could feel. He was sure if he ever looked into those eyes in person, he would either burst into flame like a match head or melt like a candle. He shook his head, hoping to break the spell she had him in, and looked at the fallen giant. He felt like David, after he'd taken down Goliath.

A steady stream of blood gushed from the flattened remains of the man's nose. He had turned while falling and landed face-first on the night stand when he went down. Blood was pouring from his mangled foot, and his ruined nose. He lay silent and motionless. Wayne knew he was still alive, or his heart wouldn't continue to pump blood from his wounds. When Wayne got closer to the fallen monster he drew a deep breath, leaned forward and watched and listened for evidence the man's body hadn't yet given up. He would need to get closer to tell for sure. With confidence bolstered by the sight of the huge man beaten and bloody on the floor, Wayne lifted himself to his hands and knees. He was in agony. The kick must have broken some ribs. After pausing to recover slightly and allow his vision to clear, he felt sufficiently clear-headed to push himself up to his knees and knee-walked to the silent figure, a wet sucking sound coming from his knees as he passed through the pool of blood. His mission was to kill the man, and he had to be sure he'd fulfilled his duty. If the huge man was not dead, Wayne would find a creative method to complete the job.

Wayne stopped when he was close enough to touch the fallen man. He cautiously reached down and pressed his fingers against the side of the man's neck, searching for a pulse. He felt nothing, though he wasn't sure he was doing it right. He tried the other side. He had no idea if there would be any reason to do so. It was all he could think of to do. He was about to give up and assume the man was dead, when the big man's eyes flew open and his fist came up and connected with Wayne's Adams apple. To keep from falling over backwards, Wayne reached out and grabbed a handful of the blood-soaked carpet.

Unbelievably, the man that only moments ago Wayne had believed was dead sat up. Wayne blinked in disbelief, and said aloud the first thing that came to mind, "What are you, a God-damn terminator?" The big man began choking, grabbed his throat and dropped again to his back, but grasped at Wayne's face, leaving finger nail gouges across his chin. Wayne glanced around the sparsely furnished room, and saw no weapon. Other than the bed and night stand, there was only the lamp, still lit, but halfway across the room, and not big enough to be a worthwhile weapon, had it been in reach.

In a move of utter desperation that he was later very proud of, Wayne bent quickly and bit into the man's neck in the same spot where, only a minute before he'd been feeling for a pulse. The rush of blood that had filled his mouth when he clamped his teeth on the man's foot paled by comparison. The blood from the fallen giant's severed jugular vein threatened to choke him. Its 98.6 temp didn't help matters at all. A mouth and throat full blood close to a hundred degrees was almost impossible to survive. He had no alternative but to swallow as much of it as he could as fast as he could to keep from drowning. The man's hand groped for his face once last time, and then dropped to the floor beside his body.

Wayne sat on the floor until the man's heart had pumped its last. Then he looked through the house till he found a bathroom. He would have no problem finding his way back to the room with the sliding door; a blind man could follow the footprints he left behind. First, he put a finger down his throat and vomited a gut full of black blood into the toilet. He took a steaming shower and stuffed his blood-soaked clothes in a linen closet, where he also found a robe. He cinched it up tight. It wasn't ideal evening wear, but it would have to do. Hopefully the darkness would keep him from being noticed. He'd be screwed if a cop stopped him for anything. He'd have to be on his best behavior driving back to the hotel. He back-tracked to the sliding door and slipped out into the night

As he started the Jeep and pulled away from the home of the dead giant, he wondered if he'd see the witch's face in his dreams that night. He sincerely hoped that if he did, it would be the beautiful face; not the terrifying one. And he hoped she would be as proud of his resourcefulness as he was. And he also hoped she'd come clean about the war she'd sent him into this night. If he'd know, he'd have gone in with a shock stick or a gun

BELADONNA

Donna Grave was, in fact, in midflight as Wayne Brogan drove away from the dead singer's home. The entire time Wayne had been struggling with the bodybuilding death-metal star she was in his head, and she knew when and how it had ended. Wayne had wondered during the confrontation if the witch knew the target was a monster. She did, in fact, know she was sending him to kill a giant. She didn't care. It would make the story of the murder all the more stupendous, *if* Brogan succeeded. If not, and Brogan was the one that died, she'd find another psycho. They were a dime-a-dozen, if you knew where to look. Donna knew where to look. While Brogan's solution to the problem wasn't a stroke of genius on his part, simply a fortunate turn of events, it made her exceedingly happy. She had told him from the beginning to make the murders as horrific and dramatic as possible; definite front-page material, so the whole world would notice. And what could be a more horrific news story than a death-metal star having his neck chewed open? And, they will probably play up the blood dinking thing. Wayne had no advance plan to kill the rocker with his teeth, and certainly had no interest in drinking his blood. Donna knew that; she'd been in his head. She'd seen that he wasn't capable of very advanced planning. They were just bonuses, for the press.

The captain announced that they were on schedule, and would be landing in Boise in approximately ninety minutes. David Boyd didn't know it yet, but his life was about to change dramatically. She had plans that depended on him; plans that had begun with one of her feelings. She never doubted her feelings. The wheels had been put in motion when Brogan drowned his son. Boyd and his dear departed son were to be her co-stars in the grand drama to come. They were essential. The other two; the drunken kid-sister, and the body-builder were collateral damage; strictly tools of misdirection. To her they were no more than a magician's beautiful assistant; only there to make people look in the wrong place. Now she had only to decide what to do with Brogan. Donna sipped a rum and coke and reclined her seat back, feeling very serene, and supremely confident of her ultimate success.

ALTER

George Alter read and reread the police reports and lab results from the Boyd boy's murder. What he'd said to John Paxton before he took off for Vegas was the absolute truth. Until Danny Boyd's death, he didn't know death-metal music existed. After watching the videos he could find on YouTube, he wasn't sure it qualified as music at all. But that was only his opinion. And his opinion was undoubtedly colored by the generation gap.

The most confusing and disturbing thing about the case, outside of a two-year old face-down in the bathtub, of course, was the timeline. The boy's grandmother helped him take a bath, and made sure he brushed his teeth. He got into his Captain America pajamas and climbed into bed. Mrs. Boyd tucked him in and kissed him goodnight at 8:30 p.m. That was the last time she saw him alive. When he wasn't in his bed at 5:00 a.m., she searched the house and found his body floating in a foot of water in the tub.

Sometime between 8:30 p.m. and 5:00 a.m. somebody came in the house and killed the boy. It was done silently and efficiently. It was the type of murder that would be easy, and come off perfectly in a novel or a made for TV movie. But in the real world, with no script, it wouldn't be so easy. For one thing, when it comes to a grandchild, a grandmother's ears are like a bat's ears; they hear everything. Plus, it was a clear night; so, the yard he; or she, Alter corrected himself, had to cross from the alley behind the house to the back door would have been bathed in bright moonlight. With a house on each side of Mrs. Boyd's and more houses across the alley, the killer would have to be really lucky to make it across the yard unnoticed. Every neighborhood has a night owl or insomniac awake during the night. Also, the agents assigned to canvasing the neighborhood were assured by the nosy resident across the street from Mrs. Boyd had found that two neighbors within earshot of Mrs. Boyd's home had dogs that were outside every night. Neither of them had barked during the night Danny was killed. Both of the dog owners had assured the agents that no one moving around the neighborhood at night, especially a stranger, would have escaped their dogs' notice.

Alter had discovered during the investigation that in response to complaints of prowlers over the several weeks prior to the murder; a police car had been circling the neighborhood every hour on the hour. So, the murderer had escaped being noticed by the grandmother, the busybody neighbor, the two dogs and a police car patrolling the neighborhood hourly. Which meant the murderer was the luckiest son of a bitch on the planet, or knew things nobody could know.

He supposed it was possible that the murder was a random act perpetrated by the recently reported prowler. But the coincidence of David Boyd's son being murdered after Boyd saved a woman from an attacker whose DNA matched that of a known rapist and murderer was simply too great. He had no doubt the murder was an act of revenge, and he knew Paxton felt the same.

Though George Alter knew there was something especially unnerving about the case; even beyond somebody drowning a child, the word supernatural never crossed his mind. He had no idea what was to come.

PAXTON

John Paxton sat across a desk from Doctor Marcus Ryan; the Chief Medical Examiner for Clark County, Nevada. He'd been awake most of the night reading the police report about Sandy Tate's death by screwdriver. He was desperate to prove or disprove a link between Sandy Tate and Davey Boyd. Like George Alter, he couldn't buy the coincidence of two different killers killing family members of death-metal singers in less than two weeks. The distance between Boise and Las Vegas wasn't great enough to slow down a dedicated serial killer. And that's just what he was convinced they were dealing with. He hoped he was wrong. Sadly, in too many instances when tracking a serial killer, there was nothing to do but wait; wait and see who's killed next. In police procedure, a pattern isn't considered proven until a third occurrence; two could be a coincidence; no matter how much Paxton believed differently in this case. Had Agent Paxton realized how closely his thoughts mirrored Donna Grave's he would have been repulsed. The medical examiner folded his hands on his desk; his fingers interlaced and looked at Paxton silently for several moments.

"You've seen my report?" he asked finally. John Paxton nodded.

"Nasty stuff," the M.E. said. Paxton nodded again. "What did you find?"

"I've been doing this a long time." He stopped, the unfinished sentence seeming to hang in the air between them. Paxton didn't know what was expected of him. The awkward silence stretched out.

"How long?" he asked, just to fill the quietness.

"Almost twenty-eight years. And it still sickens me."

"I'd think you'd have developed a pretty strong stomach by now."

The doctor shrugged. "It's not my stomach. My stomach's fine. I still can't get my mind around it."

"Around murder?"

"No. I've seen plenty of murder; more than one person should ever have to see, I think. But whoever did this did it twice." The doctor really sounded sick.

"I don't understand." Paxton said honestly. The doctor pushed back from his desk and stood up. "Do you want to see? Her body hasn't been claimed yet. I understand the brother signed himself into rehab; a guilt response I suppose. He was so wasted when she was killed, someone could have driven a truck into his house and he wouldn't have known it."

Paxton shook his head. "Do I need to see?"

"No," the doctor answered. He sat back down at his desk. "You know how she was killed?"

Paxton nodded.

"Somebody put a screwdriver in her left ear." A sad, exasperated sigh escaped him, like it had been waiting for a chance to escape when he stopped speaking. Before speaking again, the doctor made a sound that was every bit as exasperated and sad. It seemed to be the day for sad sighs.

"The girl was fifteen and small for her age. That was the first clue."

"Clue!"

"It was my first clue that he'd done it twice."

Paxton was growing impatient. "Done what twice?"

"The bastard thrust the screwdriver in her ear twice. He wanted to make sure she was dead."

"How do you know he did it twice?"

"I've been doing this job for twenty-eight years this May."

Paxton prodded him along, "Doctor, please tell me what you're talking about."

"In twenty-seven odd years, I've never seen such a case of over-kill. Paxton waited.

"When I arrived at the scene, the screwdriver was still in the victim's ear. Thank God the first responders didn't remove it. The handle of the screwdriver was protruding from the victim's head at a nearly perfect ninety-degree angle. The tip of the blade was protruding more than an inch from the other ear. On a larger person the blade might not have been long enough for that to happen. Getting that to happen wouldn't require a physics degree but it would require concentration. I didn't discover till I got into the autopsy that that wound wasn't the cause of death.

"What?" What do you mean?"

"The thrust that went clear through her head was a second blow. The screwdriver had already been driven in her ear once. When I looked inside, I could follow the wound-path. The first time the screwdriver entered her ear at an upward angle. She may have seen her attacker, and was pulling away. That would explain the angle of entry. The point of the blade grazed the maxillary bone and was stopped when it struck the inside of her skull behind her temple."

"Would that have been fatal?" Paxton asked.

"Oh yes."

"Then why the second stab?"

"I'm sorry, Agent Paxton, if I could answer questions like that one, I'd be on the lecture circuit, helping people like you stop people like the one that did this. The second time definitely wasn't necessary, if his only purpose was to kill the girl."

"Could it have been torture?"

"Doubtful. She would have been dead very quickly after the first thrust. The amount of blood loss would have been huge. Even if she was still alive when the second thrust was made, she'd have lost consciousness, and would have felt nothing. If I had to guess…" the doctor stopped.

"Please, Doctor Ryan, guess."

"I think it was just for entertainment; for pure enjoyment."

"Why? How could you know that?"

"The first thrust, the one that went in at an angle and struck the inside of her skull."

"Yes?"

"You are aware that bruising sometimes becomes visible even after the victim is dead?" the doctor asked.

Paxton nodded.

"That thrust wasn't made with enough force for the point to do any significant damage to the inside of her skull. Also, there was no apparent bruising on her ear where the hilt of the handle would have impacted. So, the evidence shows that the first thrust was done somewhat hesitantly. "No," the doctor corrected himself, "That's probably not the best way to describe it; unsurely would be a better word. The viciousness of the murder indicates the killer is not new to performing violent acts; but it was probably his first experience at driving a weapon in someone's ear. The first thrust would have been fatal; of that, I'm sure. But the second thrust; the one that penetrated her head entirely was much more forceful. If the diameter of the handle had been half as large, at least a portion of its length would also have entered her ear canal. The second thrust was done more enthusiastically. That's the only word I can think of. I imagine that a psychologist would make some sort of insightful sexual tie-in at this point. I'm no psychologist, though I have consulted with many over the course of my career, but my gut feeling is that he did it the second time because he really liked it the first time. And, as I said, at least a small amount of care was required to control the angle of the thrust. I'm glad I can't get into this person's head; it would probably be a very frightening place; but he may have derived pleasure from seeing the tip of the weapon protruding from her other ear. The ultimate penetration, you might say."

DAVID

David lifted the guitar from the two-pegged hanger on the bedroom wall. When he'd initially hung it there, Patty stood back and looked on proudly. Not proud of the guitar, but of him; for multiple reasons. He'd signed the recording contract just a week before, but he wasn't especially excited. The other guys in the band were absolutely ecstatic about it, but David hadn't been nearly as thrilled. Instead of acting like it was a goal attained, or a pinnacle reached, he seemed like a person resigned to a situation, as a man who doesn't like his job would act when he left for work in the morning. She knew he wasn't proud of being successful at playing music he hated. Now, as he slipped the ends of the strap over the chrome pegs on the guitar's body, he recalled the smile of contentment on her face that day. Earlier, over breakfast, he'd commented that once the album came out, and the tour contract was finalized, they could afford a nicer place. She'd told him, in no uncertain terms, that she was very happy where they were, and had no desire to move. Then, she'd told him she was pregnant.

The happiness he remembered from that day wasn't because of the contract, the album, an upcoming tour, his writing credits, and certainly not because of the new guitar.

What he remembered from that day was that he was incredibly happy simply because Patty was happy. And; at that point he still believed in happily ever after. That was then, this was now. Now he knew happily ever after was just a pipe-dream.

His mind never stopped churning; churning with thoughts of what might have been. He'd never come to grips with losing patty; the sheer suddenness of it. It was like having a rug pulled out from under your whole life. The rug was your support; something you always knew would be there to support you; then it was gone, in the blink of an eye. Except you could always get a new rug.

Then one day, while he was watching the garbage truck make its noisy turn around, the doorbell rang, and there was his old friend, Special Agent Paxton. And Danny was dead, and his mother was in the hospital, curled up in a fugue state. If it had been a movie, he would have at least been doing something worthwhile when the bell rang; like nursing a baby bird with a broken wing back to health, or writing a children's book. But he was watching the garbage truck. It felt like Davey deserved more.

His mother had for the most part, become herself again, though she sometimes slipped into periods of total silence, saying nothing, but the set of her creased brow showing intense concentration. Wondering what she'd done wrong, that brought on Davey's death; and what she should have done different. It was the same mental quick-sand David had slogged his way through time and again after Patty was cut in half along a highway, where he should have been, pulling on a tire iron. At least he'd had the luxury of knowing what he'd done wrong. His mother had done nothing wrong, and may never come to grips with the fact; she'd done everything right, and still lost her grandson.

David remembered something his mother told him back when he'd first gotten the confirmation of the recording contract. He'd told her about the engagement ring he already had picked out, and how he was going to buy Patty a new house, and an SUV; something more rugged, in case of an accident. And maybe travel. Neither of them had grown up with money, as his mother well knew, and neither had ever been outside the States. His plans weren't lavish; just simple rewards for hard work. Still, his mother had said a perfectly motherly thing. She put her hand on his and said, "David; man plans, and God laughs." It wasn't meant to be a buzz-kill. It was her version of; "Don't count your chickens."

David put the strap on the guitar, black strap on a black guitar, of course; chosen to fit the image of darkness necessary to be in a successful death-metal band. His amp waited in the corner of the bedroom. There was no place else to put it in the little house. It was another inconvenience that most wives would have bitched about, but that Patty took as a matter of course. She said if he was an accountant, the corner would be filled with a computer desk or file cabinets. David's intention in lifting the black guitar down was to see if he could play some real music, like the old days. Though he'd gotten sick to death of playing the song years ago, Free Bird would feel wonderful right now. He wasn't sure he wanted to plug the guitar in. Trying to play the big amp at low volume was like trying to drive a Ferrari legally through a school zone. The machine wasn't designed that way.

He'd never been especially good at multi-tasking, but he'd developed a knack for dwelling on the past; specifically past miseries, no matter what else he was doing. Now he sat on the side of the bed with the guitar propped on his lap. He'd decided to pass on the amp, so the music he made came out soft and soothing. Soon the multi-tasking began. His hands continued making music, moving as though on auto-pilot. They were indeed siphoning Free Bird from his fatigued brain. But the other part of his mind went elsewhere; to the very places he never again wanted it to go. For some reason, the thing that arose in the forefront of his mind was what his mother had said; about man planning and God laughing. This time, as the misery of his recent life played out in his head like a movie on fast forward-he listened for God's laughter. He wondered if it would sound as phony as the canned laughter that permeated the foolishness on "I Love Lucy" or any of the other hundreds of sit-coms that weren't funny enough to draw real laughs. After endless hours of listening for holy laughter, he decided that if he heard it, it proved that God was someone he didn't want to hang around with. David placed the guitar on the bed and picked up the phone. Sitting around the house was driving him mad. He had no choice but to get back on stage. If nothing else, the noise would drown out God's laughter.

PASE BEHIND BARS
DAY 1

Franklin Pace stood, bewildered, staring through cold steel bars, painted a shiny battleship-gray. He was praying that any moment a guard would come tell him that his bail was paid and he was free to go, but not to leave Fresno. The don't leave Fresno part was a scene planted in his head by years of TV police shows, where Joe Friday or Steve McGarett or some other equally severe cop laid down the law to some nefarious, clearly guilty lawbreaker. The difference in his case from the cop shows was that he'd done nothing illegal, especially not since he got to Fresno. Of course, he felt sure every person arrested claimed innocence. He would be glad to abide by the 'don't leave town' rule if it got him out of this cell. The closest he'd ever come to doing anything illegal in the past, except for speeding and fudging on his taxes, was a few questionable business deals; but nothing out of the ordinary in the agent business.

He'd been dressing to go out and grab a nice meal, courtesy of his largest client; Donna Grave. A knock had come at his hotel room door. Almost immediately a more forceful pounding followed it. By the time he had his pants pulled up and went stumbling toward the door, trying to zip up as he went, a loud, demanding voice shouted from the hall,

"Franklin Pace! Open the door and come out slowly, with your hands behind your head!"

When he'd done as he was told, his second step hadn't made solid contact with the soft, beautiful carpet in the hotel hall. It was Donna that told him to choose a really nice hotel, and the tab would be on her. That fact kept sticking in the front of his mind, and had been ever since the cell door slammed behind him. It was a confusing situation from the start. Donna had more money than she could ever spend, but she wasn't one to throw it around; at least for somebody else's enjoyment. For her to call him out of the blue and tell him to take a road trip at her expense there must be a way she'd benefit. She surely didn't suddenly decide he looked tired and needed a break. Yet, here he was. He couldn't do Donna or anyone else any good behind bars. But then again, she had basically told him to live it up, but to keep the receipts. She'd even pointed out the benefits of paying with plastic.

About the hundredth time he replayed the events leading up to his being behind bars, it dawned on him that it was almost as though she'd wanted him to leave a trail of his movements in Fresno. And the thing she had told him about thinking of her when he got there and he'd know what to do. It had been true. He'd never been to Fresno in his life, but he'd known just what hotel to go to, which restaurants to eat at, what stores to shop at, everything, as though someone was in his head directing his movements.

Now, staring out through the bars, feeling totally helpless, he wondered why she hadn't come to his rescue. His one phone call had been to her. He had a law degree, but only in civil law, and it was an online degree. He had no clue who to call for criminal representation. So, his only call had been to her. All he'd gotten was her voice-mail, itself a major production, in her best, most sultry voice, backed by a string quartet playing Bolero. He was surprised, not at the message; but that she hadn't answered. He'd arranged for the quartet and found just the right musical arrangement for the message himself. It was only one of the dozens of outwardly ridiculous things he'd been directed to do as her manager. Another thing he'd personally arranged for her was the feature that directed all incoming calls to her mobile phone if not answered by five rings. She was so attention- hungry that she never left home without her phone. She didn't want to risk missing an opportunity for notoriety. That only left the conclusion that she knew it was him calling and chose not to answer.

Standing at the bars, trembling with a nauseating mixture of fear and frustration, he made a decision; Best client or not, great ass or not; he was done with her. No more Belladonna for him. The decision gave him no satisfaction at all. He was pretty sure she was already done with him.

Finally, nearly an hour after the cell door clanged shut, one of the detectives who'd arrested him came to the cell, handcuffed him behind his back and led him to a desk. He pointed to a metal folding chair across the desk and Pace sat down, the cuffs rattling against the back of the chair. He jumped at the sound, and shifted his position on the chair. The detective simply smiled; presumably having seen it all before. The detective's first question took him by surprise.

"Have you ever been to Boise?"

"Yeah."

"When?"

Pace paused to think, and then said "Three years ago. September, I think."

"You weren't there three weeks ago?"

"No, I haven't been there for three years." Pace tried his best to sound firm, but sincere. "What's going on here?"

"You've been in Fresno for two days." It was more a statement than a question. There was little doubt the man was confident his statement was accurate, and needed no confirmation. Still, Pace felt that his answer could be very important. Finally, he said, "Yes, two days."

"Here on business?"

"No, just a break from work."

"How about last week? Did you happen to be on a break from work in Las Vegas?"

"I haven't been to Vegas in months!" Pace was nearing panic. "What's this all about? Do I need an attorney?" he nearly screamed. The detective narrowed his eyes, and calmly asked,

"I don't know, do you?"

"What am I under arrest for?"

Again, as calmly as if he were discussing last night's episode of Survivor, the detective said, "Suspicion of murder."

Pace started crying. "Murder! That's insane! You're insane! Who am I supposed to have murdered?"

The detective remained utterly calm, showing no indication he was angered, or impressed by Pace's outburst. He stared Pace in the eyes, as motionless as the hands of a clock. Finally, he said, "Gary Layne. You ever heard of him?"

Pace shook his head vehemently. "No, never! Who's he?"

"Well, till two nights ago, he was the singer for a band. A band called 'Impaler.' Ever hear of them?"

"No!"

"You've never heard of the band, or the singer? I thought with you being in show business, and all, you may have heard of them."

Pace shook his head so violently, tears flew.

"Maybe you know him by his stage name; Vlad. You know, like Vlad the Impaler. It's really creative if you think about it, isn't it?"

Pace looked at the ceiling, and shook his head. "No. I've never heard of him," he whined.

The detective plowed on, ignoring the fact that Pace appeared ready to faint.

"Two nights ago, somebody chewed into his neck till they opened his jugular vein and he bled out. Does that ring any bells?"

Pace's eyes rolled back in his head, and he felt faint. As he passed out, he heard laughter in his head, feminine and chilling, and he knew he was through.

When Franklin Pace came to at first, he thought it had all been an especially bad nightmare. Then he discovered he was still in front of the detective's desk. Only now he was on the floor between the desk and the chair he'd been seated in. The first voice he heard was that of the detective; who'd been grilling him. He was a man of few words, "Get up, you piece of shit!"

Pace shook his head. He was sure his brain was sliding around in his head. He felt detached from reality. He remembered what had been happening before he blacked out, but remembering wasn't the same thing as believing. The detective, whose name he still didn't know strode purposefully around the desk, grabbed Pace under his arms, and hoisted him roughly up onto the chair. He stayed behind him only long enough to see that he wasn't going to slide to the floor a second time. Then he went around the desk, practically at a run and sat back down.

"You think you can stay in the chair?" Pace nodded. He asked what on the surface seemed like a ridiculous question, but he had a right to know.

"What in the hell is your name?"

"Detective Raymond Cray," not that it's any of your business. I don't normally share personal information with murderers!" He said it forcefully, plainly certain that, at least in his mind, he was perfectly right. Pace's fear took a back seat to wonderment. "I don't know what the hell you're talking about. Shit! You don't know what you're talking about! I didn't kill anybody!" What makes you think I killed this Layne guy?

"Well, he's real damn dead!" Cray growled.

"I didn't make him that way! Please explain what's going on." Pace was whimpering again. He knew it and hated himself for it. Hell, he was an agent, and agents don't whimper. Agents take charge. If there was one thing an agent always knew, of at least acted like, was that he was the smartest person in the room. Now he felt like the dumbest person on earth.

Detective Cray picked up a brown folder, held closed by a piece of string looped around plastic discs on the envelope's surface. He opened it and shook out three stacks of papers, each pound securely with a large binder clip. Before doing anything farther with the bound sheets, he laid them in a semi-circle, like three cards spread fan-shaped before a dealer. Detective Cray froze, favoring Franklin Pace with the thousand-yard stare of a man who'd just produced proof of his claims. Using a common intimidation method, he bent closer to Pace and said, "You've been on quite a spree, haven't you?" He waved his hand over the papers like a magician performing slight-of-hand before speaking again. He offered a thin, insincere smile. He was acting marginally more civil and while definitely not friendly, possibly more willing to listen. When he spoke again, he spoke slowly, giving the sound of each word time to fade suitably from the air before going on to the next word, thereby punctuating each word with the proper significance.

"Gary Layne was attacked and killed in his home two nights ago. That's the same day you arrived in Fresno, is it not?" Price nodded, praying it was the right thing to do.

"Based on time of death, we estimate Layne died between one and two a.m. It looked like he put up one hell of a fight. And whoever killed him was either very tough or real damned determined." Cray paused, watching Price for any sign of a response. Seeing nothing but fear, he went on, "This Layne guy was huge; six-three, two eighty-five. It seems his hobby was bodybuilding. Still seeing nothing useful on Price's face, he continued.

"We assume the killer wasn't aware of the fact, since there was no weapon involved. I wouldn't have taken the guy on unarmed. I guess all the muscles made him look more intimidating on stage. Impaler is a death-metal band." Again, he read nothing in Pace's countenance except confusion. "You familiar with it?"

Price mumbled, "What?"

"Death-metal. You know what it is?" The detective's impatience was growing.

"No," Price answered truthfully.

"It's music where all they sing about is death, murder, suicide; That kind of shit."

Price took advantage of a lull in Cray's fuming. "What does that have to do with me?"

Cray finally got down to the crux of the matter, "We got a call on our tip line that we should check you out."

"A tip from who?"

"Anonymous. She's the one most of our tips come from. If it's not Ms. Anonymous, it's Mr. Anonymous.

Price thought about the chilling laughter he was sure he'd heard in his head. "She" What did her voice sound like?"

"Damned if I know. I didn't take the call. One of the tip line volunteers took it. We get at least a hundred calls a day. Fresno ain't L.A. but it ain't Mayberry, either. We get way more than our share of crime, and criminals. He unclipped one of the stacks of paper and flipped to the second or third sheet. "It says here that the call came in two days ago; the day you got here, at two pm. It was a woman who told us all about you. She told us where you'd be staying, what you look like and that you'd be driving an Enterprise rental; a red metal-flake Mustang convertible with Texas plates. We found you right where she said we would, you look like she said you would, and the keys to the Mustang were on the nightstand." Detective Cray smiled, but it was really more of a sneer. "The car was over- parked. That's a ten dollar fine, but we'll talk about that some other time."

"And she didn't give her name?" Pace was on the verge of collapse.

"I told you the call was anonymous!" Cray was getting angrier by the second.

"Did the person who took the call say anything about how she sounded? Was there anything strange about her?"

"What do you think our volunteers are, counselors? This isn't Alcoholics Anonymous or a suicide hotline. These people answer phones and pass the information on to a cop.

Pace was now pleading, "Do you know who took the call?

"Yes, I do. But you're not going to. I've already told you more than you have a right to know." Cray pushed a button on the phone on his desk.

A disembodied voice answered, "Yes sir?"

"Come take this guy back to holding."

A uniformed policeman came and took him back to the cell with the cold gray bars.

PACE BEHIND BARS
DAY 2

Detective Cray sat at his desk. Again, Franklin Pace sat across from him. Again, his hands were cuffed behind him. The only thing different was that the chair he sat in was more substantial, and had arms; hopefully to keep Pace from crumbling to the floor, should he faint again.

Cray stared at Pace levelly, trying again to read his expression. He saw nothing more than he had the day before. He stared for a long time. Pace didn't fidget; only stared back. Overnight he'd regained some of his inherent agent bravado.

The detective said, "Mister Price, I must say you look more together today."

"Thanks."

"Don't take that to mean I think you're any less guilty. All I mean is you don't look like you're ready to piss your pants today."

"Overnight I decided that an innocent man has nothing to fear." Cray lowered his head, but kept his eyes cast upwards at Price's face. He didn't say anything, but his mind was racing. It was nothing he'd admit to Price; in fact had a difficult time admitting it to himself, tip or no tip, his gut didn't tell him Price was guilty. It also didn't tell him Price was innocent. He found something unnerving about Price when he tried to read his face; almost like there was another face behind it; hiding.

Still, his uncertainty had made him ignore protocol. In the middle of the night, he'd made a call to the Police Chief. The chief wasn't too happy about being awakened, but heard him out. What Cray asked for was unheard of, but the chief had enough past experience with Cray's positive results to give him the go-ahead.

Ten minutes after Pace was brought to the detective's office a rap came on the door. Cray said, "Come in," and a young man, no more than seventeen, in jeans and a tee shirt came in and took a chair that Cray directed him to. Cray looked at Pace, and said, "Pace, this is Eddie Dean. He's the volunteer who took the call that led us to arrest you. You've got five minutes. Make them count. Pace looked confused. "Ask your questions".

Pace was stunned, and stared slack-jawed at the detective. "Cray glanced at a clock on the wall and said, "Four minutes and fifty seconds." Price turned toward Eddie Dean and sat with his mouth open for a few seconds, unsure where to start. He knew what he wanted to ask, but the situation was so crazy he didn't know where to start. Finally, he said,"You took the call?" Eddie Sean nodded. "It was a woman?" Again, Dean nodded.

"What did she sound like?"

"What"

Price didn't know what to ask. He looked at Detective Cray, who'd been looking back and forth at them, like a man watching a tennis match. Cray nodded, and said, "Time's a wastin'." Before he could ask anything else, Eddie said, "Kind of sultry. The kind of voice a guy always hopes to hear. I never heard anybody sound like that before." "Was her voice deep, or high?" "Kind of low." Then Eddie Dean said something that made Price feel both hopeful and panicky; "It was a little rough. It reminded me of the sound a cat makes when it's purring."

Pace jumped. "Cray said, unpleasantly, "You're not going to fall out of the chair, are you?" Price shook his head, and again focused on Eddie Dean. "Did she have an accent?"

"Not really, at least not that I remember. Is that important?"

"I guess not." Pace was again stumped for another question to ask. Before he came up with one, Eddie Dean said, "There was one crazy thing."

Cray said, "Go on". Now Eddie was at a loss for words. Both Cray and Pace were staring at him like men anxious to hear the punch-line of a great joke.

"Well, when she talked, it was like the words spilled over."

"Cray asked, "What?"

"Well, even though I had the phone tight up against my ear…I had to because it was twelve and a lot of people were leaving for lunch, and chatting back by the door. It was pretty noisy. I could hear her from the phone just fine, but even when things got louder around me, I could hear her perfectly. That's what I mean when I said the words spilled over; it felt like her voice was coming out of the phone and soaking right into my head." Franklin Pace again jumped. This time he did feel like he might fall from the chair. He took a deep breath and asked, "And she told you I killed this Gordon Tate?"

Eddie Dean nodded. "Him and a girl in Vegas; some singer's sister, and another singer's kid in Boise." "Was that all she said?" This time Detective Cray asked the question. Eddie Dean looked thoughtful. "No, she said, "You'll dream of me."

"You'll dream of me?"

"Yeah, you'll dream of me. And I did."

"You didn't happen to dream up her name, did you?" Cray asked sarcastically. "Or what she looks like?" Dean shifted uncomfortably in his chair. "No sir, I don't know her name, but she's beautiful." Detective Cray snickered derisively, but Franklin Price practically jumped out of his skin. "What did she look like?" If his hands wouldn't have been cuffed behind him, he would have grabbed Dean and pulled the young man's face up into his own. "What did she look like?"

"It was just a dream," Eddie Dean said, frightened that he'd done something wrong. He looked at Detective Cray. Cray nodded. Eddie said, somewhat hesitantly, "She had a narrow face; sort of heart shaped like Olivia Wilde. She had full lips, and sort of looked like she might have dimples if she smiled. But I got the feeling she doesn't smile much. Her hair was short and black. Her eyes were big and green and shone like cat's eyes do at night if your headlights hit them, but they were kind of spooky; like they were shining in pure blackness." Franklin Pace wobbled in his chair. Detective Cray noticed, but said nothing about it. He looked at Eddie Dean and said, "You sound like an article in People Magazine."

Eddie Dean shrugged, and said, "You asked." Detective Cray said, "Thank you for coming in, Mister Dean, and of course, thank you for your volunteer work. We'll contact you if there's anything else." The young man shook the detective's hand, then extended his hand toward Pace, but pulled it back awkwardly when he remembered the handcuffs.

Eddie Dean was probably less than twenty feet down the hall beyond the door before Detective Cray said, "Okay Pace, was that supposed to prove anything I don't already know? All I know now is that a volunteer kid fell in love with a mystery woman who probably makes a living doing phone sex." Pace asked, "Why did you do that. Is that routine, letting a suspect talk to a witness? Assuming I'm still a suspect, that is."

"You're still a suspect. I haven't found anything to prove you're guilty yet, but that doesn't prove you're innocent. I just wanted to check out what he had to say."

"Any particular reason?" "No," Detective Cray said. "Just idle curiosity." I'm usually pretty good at reading people, but you're hard to read. Either you're really scared shitless, or you've had a lot of practice at hiding what you're thinking. This was only another opportunity to observe, and see what makes you hard to read."

"For what it's worth, both things are true. I'm a talent agent, hiding what I'm thinking is what I do every day. And, I _am_ scared shitless."

"Okay, Pace. One more question. When he described his mystery woman, you jumped like you'd been stung in the ass by a wasp. Why?"

"I know who she is. And she's the reason I'm in Fresno."

"Tell me about her." The statement was unremarkable and generally forgettable; certainly not the words Detective Raymond Cray would have chosen to be his last. As Franklin Pace watched dumbfounded, the detective's eyes rolled impossibly far back in his head. If, at that point, the cop could still see, all he would be seeing was the inside of his brain. It happened with no warning, and so suddenly Pace couldn't believe his own eyes. Cray's eyeballs literally spun back, like a rolling ball in a pinball machine. Cray didn't make a sound, but he did manage to slap his hands to his temples. Blood ran from his eyes, making his eyeballs look as though they were floating in their sockets. Gradually some thin sludge that could only be brain matter became visible in the twin blood streams. Pace tried to go to the man, though he had no idea what he could do for him. It didn't look like a situation where C.P.R. would help. It was a moot point, anyway; he couldn't have performed C.P.R. with his hands cuffed behind him. It lasted less than a minute. The detective fell forward; his face coming to rest on the thin stack of clipped-together papers, still lying on his desk where he'd placed them the day before. There was a sound Franklin Pace was certain he'd never forget; whether he spent the rest of his days behind bars or not. Cray's eyes had bled so copiously that there was a horrible wet noise; accompanied by a muted crunch: probably the sound of his nose breaking; an injury he'd never know about, or care about.

Pace struggled with the cuffs again, but it quickly became clear it was a waste of effort, and time. He wanted to get someone; to let someone know what had happened to Cray. Even though the man had been in charge of the effort to put him away, probably for life, nobody deserved to die like that.

On the way into the office, he'd seen how stout the door was, and he'd heard the solid "thunk" it had made when Eddie Dean pulled it shut behind him. There was a lot of noise beyond the door; the daily routine of the police department in a large city. A lot of voices were mingled with the sounds of doors being opened and closed. The unintelligible babble of important law enforcement information coming from a radio cut through the noise. Underlying it all was Supertramp doing 'Bloody Well Right.' Somebody out there was a fan of classic rock. It was turned up pretty loud, probably so the people out there could hear over the other work day noise. Cray knew his yelling would go unnoticed; unless someone happened to be walking by the door. He began pitching his weight back and forth, till he finally toppled off the chair. He considered very briefly as he headed for the carpet that it was a good thing his hands were only cuffed behind his back, and not behind the back of the chair. He started crawling toward the door. He spared a look back at Cray. He couldn't see the man; his view blocked by the desk. He could see his shoes, now covered with blood that had run off the desk. He wondered if, when they came in, they would immediately shoot him, thinking he was somehow responsible. He made it to the door, rolled to his back, and started kicking the door with both feet, as hard as he could. To him, the sound was huge; but from the other side he had no idea.

Finally, after what seemed like forever to him, but surely wasn't more than half a minute; the door swung open and hit his feet; which were cocked for another blow. It rolled him to his side, twisting his bound hands painfully behind his back, nearly dislocating his shoulder.

Donna listened carefully, not to external sounds but to the voices in her head; thoughts, actually. She focused most easily on Franklin Pace's. It was a matter of familiarity. She'd been in his head since the day they'd met, always with an eye towards the future. Donna always watched for the right opportunity. If someone had to suffer; so be it. She'd felt no animosity toward the detective; killing him was a means to an end. Now there could be no doubt in the eyes of the police that Franklin Pace was a killer. They wouldn't be able to figure out how, but after the detective was autopsied, and no explanation was found for what happened to him, to only possibility would be that Pace was responsible. When Eddie Dean left Cray's office, he'd been fine. She didn't care if they ever figured out that she'd told Detective Cray's brain it was time to explode. She'd always wondered if it was something she could do; and now she knew. Knowing made her happy. One more tool in her bag of tricks. The detective had to die; it wasn't something she'd envisioned when she put the series of events in motion. But as it worked out, it was a perfect turn of events. The more the authorities focused on Franklin Pace, the more smoothly her plan would go. If Pace spent the rest of his life in prison, it had to be. Her reasons were beyond anything a normal person could understand, or believe.

ALTER

The more time George Alter spent trying to explain Davey Boyd's murder, the more he felt it was unexplainable. Not the perfect crime, but the impossible crime. On the surface it seemed pretty clear-cut: somebody broke into the home of the boy's grandmother, and drowned him in the bathtub. But the killer had either been unbelievably lucky, or clairvoyant. If there was an organization for the promotion, and advancement of common sense, Alter could be their poster child. But here, there was the added twist of David Boyd's past altercation with the wasted psycho eight years before. That made him the perfect candidate for a revenge attack. But why his son instead of him? And then the second incident occurred in Vegas, where Paxton now was. The chances of two attacks involving death-metal stars being a coincidence were phenomenal. Especially with them being only a week apart.

He was sitting at his computer, where he'd spent the majority of his time since Paxton left for Las Vegas. He knew that becoming obsessed with a case was always a danger; especially when dealing with such a horrendous case. He'd been receiving information on the second murder every day. As soon as John found out anything he would send the information. The second murder had been every bit as brutal as the first; if anything, more so. Davey Boyd's murder still seemed more atrocious, simply because the victim was little more than an infant. The more defenseless the victim, the more terrible the violence seemed. The second victim was only a child; a fifteen-year-old girl could do little more than run, if she had the chance that was. But with the amount of alcohol she had in her system, she could have probably only made it a few steps before falling down. So, assuming it was the same perpetrator in both cases, which George did, he only attacked helpless targets. That showed he was going after a specific victim in each case; And that he was a coward. The increasing violence could well point to a novice; feeling more and more powerful and more in control with each kill. But that made it seem even stranger; the targeting of individuals, rather than any person he might encounter indicated someone who was being directed; acting under orders, from a dominant figure. And whoever was doing the directing may have a hit list. He only hoped they could get a step ahead of him before it was too late for someone else.

Almost as if on cue, his phone chirped, indicating he'd received a text message. He always kept it lying next to his keyboard within easy reach. It was from Paxton, and was only a few words; "there's another one."

George immediately went on his computer to the information John had sent. His first glance at the included pictures reinforced his observation about the killer's escalating viciousness. He knew what the weapon had been in this case before reading John's message. It wouldn't take a trained detective to recognize teeth marks. And a dental impression wouldn't help convict the murderer here. The man's neck looked like he'd been chewed up by a meat grinder. According to John's message; the only thing that could be helpful in this case was that the victim was a big man and had gone down fighting. His attacker left a lot of his own blood behind.

So tired his vision was blurry, George Alter went home, hoping for a good night's rest, so he could look at things with fresh eyes in the morning. Unfortunately, hoping didn't make it so. Before lying down, he made a preemptive strike; three fingers of single malt scotch, straight up, with no ice. Arthur Godfrey, whom he barely recalled seeing on television as a child, was reputed to have said that hangovers are caused by stale ice. George had enough horrible thoughts and images in his head. He had no desire to top them off with a hangover.

Finally, after the green numbers glowing on the clock beside his bed said it was two a.m., he drifted off into an uneasy, fitful sleep filled with disturbing dreams; very disturbing. His alarm went off at six, as always. He didn't usually recall his dreams, but despite the lack of sleep the previous night's images were fresh in his mind. Though the dreams had awakened him several times, once on the verge of screaming, he didn't recognize till morning that there had been three distinct dreams, not just an unclear blur. The dreams had been like scenes from a play; all with different backgrounds, and each with its own subplot. Like in a play, they were also building toward a climax. It was something he knew, without there being an explanation for his knowing. The sense in which the dream's similarity to a play ended was the cast. Each individual dream featured just two characters; the first dream being only Davey Boyd, and a large figure bending over him, holding his tiny body under water. The boy's arms were flailing, searching for something, or someone to hold onto, someone to save him. In the dream George saw Davey's mouth opening and closing; either gasping for air or trying to scream. But no sound came out, and nothing went in but water. Soon, the little arms stopped flailing, and the boy's mouth ceased opening and closing. That was when George sat up in the bed, himself gasping for breath, feeling as though his lungs were filling with water; and biting down on a scream. It was unnecessary, as no one would hear the scream if he let it escape. He was afraid that his own scream would frighten him more.

His second dream was just as vivid as the first, and if anything; more hideous, due to the blood and gore involved. Still, he found it less disturbing, and infuriating than Danny's death. He felt almost as though he'd known the child, because of all his time spent studying the case.

A beautiful teenaged girl crouched on her knees in the center of a large bed. She had the covers clutched in front of her, desperate for any sort of shield. The dim glow of a night-light was the room's only illumination. It was a plastic Miss Piggy, glowing a pale pink. It was the sort of thing a girl her age would soon outgrow, if she got the chance to grow older. Her eyes were wide and frightened. She was wearing baggy boxer shorts and a t-shirt with a depiction of a black cross standing on a hill with thunder clouds and lightning in the background. Across the image, in jagged red letters was; 'CRUCIFICTION', in all capitals. She was trying to scream, but like Danny in his previous dream, no sound came from her open mouth. A large shadow fell across the terrified girl, moving closer; covering more of her by the second. The girl cowered, futilely pulling the covers over her head. In his dream, George saw a hand rip the bed covers out of the girl's small hands. Finally, she managed a scream; a sound that would follow George forever; whenever he tried to allow himself a moment of silent respite from the often-disheartening life of a homicide detective. Without letting go of the covers, another hand moved in an arc, moving slowly, deliberately. Miss Piggy's pink glow reflected off something long and slender. Then everything went a deep crimson. At the instant the color appeared, the girl's screams disappeared. George woke up kneeling in the center of his bed; the covers scrunched up in a ball in front of him like a shield. Sweat poured from his face.

The third dream was less detailed, but no less gruesome. In that dream he never really saw the victim's face, only the hideous wound inflicted by the murderer. The victim was a big man; no; more than big; huge. He was significantly larger than the man who'd killed him. But, remembering the dream in the morning, Alter thought of the shows on the Discovery channel that showed a hyena ripping open the belly of a water buffalo or hippo that was three times its size. In nature, teeth, and the willingness to use them took away a size advantage. But that was in nature. There was nothing natural about this killer.

Then there was the woman; she was something he never remembered immediately upon waking from one of the dreams. She never played a big role in the dreams; but she was always present; her face floating in the background; like a cloud, or the watermark behind the printing on a sheet of paper.

He wondered why he never remembered her being there until he'd spent time trying to analyze the dreams, and trying to come to grips with what he'd seen. He was no shrink, but he thought there was a good chance his brain was trying to protect itself from what the dream woman might mean; who she was and why she was in his head? The impression he perceived of her reason for existing in the dreams was the sense that she was overseeing the murders, or the person committing them. He had already considered the possibility that the killer was being controlled by someone with a more dominant personality; but the idea of that someone being an ethereal woman, real only in his dreams was too far out there for him to consider. He was a man of facts, and reality. But why else would she appear to be watching over the murders, like a school teacher looking over a student's shoulder to see if they're doing it right. His head swam, trying to put things together.

As George drank his morning coffee, attempting to chase the dreams from his mind, just for a while he wondered if John Paxton had been dreaming. There was no doubt; this case was the kind that seeped into you and ate away at you from the inside. Or were the dreams his to undergo alone? And why would that be? What had he done to deserve the dreams? There had to be a purpose. If so, he wasn't sure he'd want to know what it was.

PAXTON

John Paxton had no idea, as he sat in a hotel lobby in Fresno, partaking of the less than impressive complimentary continental breakfast that was so prominently promoted on the fold-out card by his bedside that George Alter was thinking about him and wondering if his sleep had also been ruined by dreams.

As he'd expected; the promised breakfast was only donuts, juice and coffee. He'd eaten little, but was on his fourth cup of coffee. He needed help waking up; he hadn't had a decent night's sleep since before leaving Las Vegas. His dreams were every bit as vivid as, but markedly different from George's.

He opened his eyes every morning, thankful the night was over. Disturbing images followed him into the waking hours. He wasn't aware of the alarming dreams that haunted George. They'd been in close contact since John left for Vegas, but had both been so wrapped up in locating the burgeoning serial killer who was at the top of their personal most-wanted lists that they hadn't had time for discussing sleep issues.

John dreamed repeatedly of a woman. She was, at the same time, the most beautiful and most frightening female he'd ever seen. She invariably appeared in the dreams surrounded by total blackness, which leant an extra layer of icy strangeness to her features. The depth of the blackness that surrounded her was in astonishing contrast to her eyes, which were the color of burning embers. Despite her beauty, her image in his head screamed evil. Each morning when the memory of the dream came to him, it was all he could do to suppress a shudder. The sensation of evil couldn't have been more real if the nightmare woman had horns.

Unbeknownst to Detective Paxton, the beautiful, yet terrifying face he saw in his dreams was the same face that appeared in Wayne Brogan's warped mind when the very thought of failure entered his head as he fought with Gary Layne, the huge singer the woman he thought of as "The Witch" had sent him to kill. Paxton wished he could project his dream to his phone so he could send it to George Alter to see if her image meant anything to him.

ALTER

The two detectives had been partners long enough that it seemed their thoughts sometimes followed the same track; like twins are known to do. Some of the other agents in the Boise office joked that they were twin sons of different mothers. It was from some old folk album from the seventies he thought. What album, he didn't know; or especially care. But it had caught on at the office, and occasionally seemed to be accurate. He didn't know at that moment if he would want it to be true or not.

BELADONNA

Things were moving along nicely. Franklin Pace was behind bars. That was the perfect place for him. He didn't deserve to be there, but that didn't concern her. He was a pawn in what was definitely the most important chess match of her life; a match she had no intention to lose.

As time went by, she was more and more amazed by her own abilities. When she'd called the Fresno police's tip line, she poured it on, and could tell by his breathing that she had the guy on the other end hooked. If she'd told him Taylor Swift chewed through Gary Layne's throat, he'd have believed her. Anybody with a thimble full of sense would know that Franklin Pace wouldn't have a snowball's chance in hell against a man like Layne. But her tip had planted the idea. And after the detective's brain had run from his eye sockets when he was alone in the room with Pace, the police would have no alternative but to look at him as a murder suspect; in both Gary Layne's murder, and Detective Cray's murder. They would have no idea how he did it, and could never prove he did. But whether he went to prison or the gas chamber her goal would be achieved; they would be focused on him. They would be distracted from her distraction.

Donna Grave followed Detective Cray's case with great interest. With her law enforcement connections, she stayed well informed. As she'd expected; all attention was focused on Franklin Pace. Just about every possible solution, and some seemingly impossible ones had been suggested; everything from Pace being infected with a fast-moving virus he breathed on the detective to voodoo. Even mind control had been suggested. When Donna heard that she'd laughed aloud. It didn't matter; while they studied Pace like a bug under a microscope, there was little or no chance they'd stumble on Wayne Brogan's connection to the murders; or hers.

PAXTON

At Boise City Airport, while walking from the FBI jet that had brought him from Fresno, John Paxton's phone rang in his brief case. An experienced luggage and phone juggler; he had no problem getting to it before the caller gave up; though he did curse at himself inwardly for not having the phone in a pocket instead of the brief case. George Alter knew he was landing about now, and he'd bet good money it was George calling. As always, he answered, "Special Agent John Paxton." He was right about who was calling. Alter said, "John?" He didn't sound just right. He sounded excited, as though there was news inside him, busting to come out.

"George," Paxton answered. He decided to forgo the usual dead Beatles reference that one or the other of them almost always mentioned when they greeted each other by their first names. Paxton asked, "What's up? Do you have to pee, or something?" He heard Alter draw a calming breath on the other end of the line.

"You first."

"Paxton said, "Okay. Whoever stuck the screwdriver in the girl's ear in Vegas is still unknown. He made clean work of it. We've got zilch to work with. The standard procedures are going on; checking motels and hotels in Vegas. Of course there are a million of them. They'll look extra close at the ones on the side of the city closest to the victim's home. They're going through license numbers and IDs on guests, and comparing them to the regulars; to see if anybody stands out. Vegas gets a lot of repeat business. I don't know if it will pay off; looking for strangers in a city where every other person is a tourist. But it's a place to start. And there's always the chance it wasn't a stranger to Vegas. I'm surprised there isn't a hit-man section in the Las Vegas Yellow Pages. Every paid informant on the strip is on the hunt. If there's a buck to be made, somebody will turn something up."

"So, how about Fresno," George quizzed him. "It looked like that guy was attacked by an alligator."

"Yeah, it was a nasty one. But we've got a better chance there."

"How so?"

"The guy left a lot of his blood behind. They're running a DNA check, but nothing yet. They are sure it's not the guy they have in custody."

"What guy?"

"That happened since I talked to you last." Paxton told Alter about Franklin Pace, and everything that had happened since his arrest.

"Franklin Pace?" George asked as if he wasn't certain he'd heard right. The excited tone was again in his voice. "From Vegas?"

"Yes, George, what is it?"

"I'm at the office. Are you coming in?" He still sounded like a kid with news he couldn't believe.

"Yeah, I'll be there in twenty minutes."

"Good." George Alter hung up.

Paxton slipped his phone in his pocket, and walked to his car. He couldn't wait to see what George was so cranked up about. The last thing he expected was to find David Boyd waiting at FBI headquarters; but when he walked in George Alter's office, David sat on the old, comfortable sofa against the wall across from the door. It was something

George had picked up at a flea market. It wasn't chosen for style or appearance, but for comfort. George had laid on it for a good ten minutes before deciding it would be a perfect addition to his office. John was with him when he picked it out and paid the lady. He also went back with him later and helped him load it in a borrowed van, and carry it into his office. George had spent many nights on the old sofa when a case kept him in the office, as had John. He was really surprised to find David waiting for him. He shook hands with David and sat beside him on the couch. It brought memories of the day he'd set beside him in his living room and told him his son was dead. He wondered if David was experiencing the same flashback. Paxton looked first at David, trying to read his state of mind, and perceived he was as restless as George had been on the phone.

"Okay, what's going on?"

David said nothing, but he seemed to be almost trembling with excitement. Finally, George Alter said, "David, why don't you explain to Agent Paxton why you came to see me." David had tears in his eyes. "I might get to talk to Davey!" He stopped speaking, leaving the confusing statement hang between them, begging for an explanation.

Paxton had come home tired, and impatient. "David, what in the hell are you talking about?" David's words began spilling out as though through a burst dam, "I got a call from a lady! She's a psychic! She said she can contact Davey, and I can talk to him!" Paxton shot Alter a questioning look. Alter shrugged; a response that offered no help or understanding at all.

Paxton asked, "George is this what you seemed so antsy about on the phone?"

"Yes, but there's more. David, tell Agent Paxton who called you."

"Her name is Donna Grave. She's a psychic." He paused to catch his breath.

"Yes, you said that. When did she contact you?"

"Last night, about nine. She says she can contact Davey!" Paxton nodded. "You said that, too. Did she say why she called you?"

David nodded hesitantly. "She read about Davey in the paper and feels bad for me, and my mom. She talked about how terrible it must have been for my mom; finding him like that." He again paused for a breath. "She told me she works with the cops a lot, as a consultant. She's helped catch killers all over the world! And if I can talk to Davey, he can tell me who killed him. He stopped for a moment, then continued, his voice calmer, but also more serious. "And he can tell me if he's happy." David paused again for breath. Paxton took advantage of the pause to ask more questions.

"I think that would be wonderful," he said, meaning every word. "But I have to ask, "David, what's in it for her? What does she want in return?" David didn't answer. Alter prodded him along. "Go on David." He sounded fatherly, but insistent. Finally, David nearly whispered, "Ten million dollars." Without a pause he continued, more fervently, "I can do that. Since the record contract, and with the albums doing so good, I can handle ten million. I could hit up the other guys in the band and come up with twice that, if I had to!"

"Did you tell her that?"

"No, that would be stupid. But I could! And I would get to talk to Davey!" He was nearly crying. Paxton looked at Alter and shrugged.

Alter said, "That's why I wanted to get your input before I told David what to do. I did some digging into Donna Grave's background. And it took longer than I expected to dig anything up. Her last name is Grave, not Graves; like I would have thought. It seems she had it legally changed when she became a celebrity. It's almost like she wanted to be harder to backtrack. But you can't hide from the Bureau. She actually does have a history of working with law enforcement."

"How about her? Does she have a record?"

She had a civil suit filed against her once for fraud. She settled out of court. I couldn't find out how much. But no criminal charges.

"What kind of law enforcement history?"

"Enough success, or luck, to make some people believe she's real. In most cases, she's allowed in because a family member of the victim or some mid-level politician insists on it. Alter paused, then added, "I suppose if you've had a family member killed or kidnapped anything looks worth a shot."

The agents had inadvertently been talking to each other, focused only on their own conversation. Alter caught himself, and said to David, "I'm sorry David; that was a terrible thing to say." David answered, "That's okay. You're right. Sometimes anything looks worth a shot." His eyes were again full of unspilled tears. He said, "Go on. I want to know what you found about her too."

Alter continued, "What I did find out about her is her manager is Franklin Pace, from Las Vegas."

"No shit?"

"Nope, No shit. That's why I was so surprised when you said he's in custody for the Fresno killing"

"Fresno?" David said, totally in the dark. He couldn't have felt more out of the loop if he were blind. "What in the hell happened in Fresno?" David asked insistently, almost angrily.

Agent Paxton explained the whole story about the Las Vegas and Fresno murders to David, with George Alter occasionally adding details where necessary. When the agents finished David asked, "Why didn't you tell me all of this. Didn't you think I had the right to know?"

Paxton answered, "David, I try very hard not to get people's hopes up till I have an idea whether a new development has any bearing on a case."

"And you think that two other death-metal singers being victims is a coincidence?"

"I'm not in the business of thinking; I'm in the business of knowing." It sounded far more insensitive than he'd intended.

"So exactly what do we know about Donna Grave?" he asked George Alter.

"I searched for her online, but just like anything you try to search online, most everything that came up was trying to sell something. There's everything from Donna Grave t-shirts to Donna Grave crystal balls and Ouija boards. I even had the chance to pre-order the 'Donna Grave' Barbie'. But, from the pictures I saw, Barbie's built like an eleven-year-old compared to her."

"So did you order the Barbie?" David asked sarcastically.

Again, Alter apologized, "Sorry David. Where did it go after she told you who she was and what she wants?"

"She gave me her phone number and I'm supposed to call her at ten tonight and tell her what I decided."

"What did you decide?" Paxton asked.

David looked stunned. "I didn't decide anything. What should I do?" he asked pleadingly. "I want to talk to Davey, but I needed to talk to you first. I don't care about the money or being made a fool of, but…"

"You don't know if you could handle the disappointment."

David nodded. "What should I do?" he asked again, looking back and forth between the two agents.

After a moment's thought, Paxton said, "Call her tonight at ten, exactly. Don't call early. If you seem too anxious, she'll think she has the upper hand. Tell her you want to do it, But you'll only give her five million up front. She gets the rest when she reaches Danny, and you get to talk to him."

David said, "You think it's a scam, don't you? You don't think she can reach Davey, do you?"

"It doesn't matter what I think. I'm just a cop trying to put facts together. But the link between this case and both her and Franklin Pace can't be a coincidence. Or if it is, it's the strangest one I've ever seen."

David looked at Alter, who nodded agreement.

"Then what" After I tell her okay, what then?

"Tell her she can say when, but you say where. Tell her you want to do whatever it is she does at your mother's house."

"Why my mother's house? She'll probably ask. What do I say?"

"Tell her you want to do it there because that's the last place you saw Davey. You feel closer to him there."

David drew a deep breath. "Well, I won't be lying. But what about my mom? What do I tell her?"

"Tell her the truth; that you want to use her house, and tell her why. But she won't be there. She'll be in the nicest hotel in Boise, courtesy of the FBI. And dinner in any restaurant that strikes her fancy."

"But, why? If this woman really can reach Davey my mom would want to be there. And why her house, anyway?"

"It's a location you chose, which makes it safer, and it will be easy to secure."

"What do you mean?"

"We've been over every inch of the house already. We know where to watch for the slightest sign of a scam, or of danger."

David looked stunned. "Danger! What danger?"

"David, we don't know what this woman is up to, but we do know her manager is mixed up in this whole mess somehow. He may not be a murderer, but somebody went to a lot of trouble to make him a suspect; which means there's a very good chance that this woman is involved in the murders somehow. And even the slightest risk is too much to subject your mother to. If Donna Grave asks why your mother isn't there, tell her she got food poisoning and was admitted to the hospital overnight for observation. We'll arrange for every hospital in the city to confirm that your mother's a patient if they get a call. This séance could turn out to be way too chancy for your mom to be involved. She'll be somewhere safe and well protected when it happens."

"Séance," David said reflectively.

"What?"

"Séance; It sounds corny, kind of Scooby doo-ish doesn't it." David looked at his hands clenched tightly in his lap, and Paxton was reminded of the day he'd had to deliver the news about Davey.

David had done the same thing then, squeezing till his knuckles were white and his fingernails were blue.

George Alter had been silent, letting David and Paxton talk things out. He now said, "There's nothing corny here David. This is something that matters to you, so it matters to us."

David reached out and shook Alter's hand. "Thank you, Agent Alter," David said sincerely. "Thank you both."

"Call me George; all my friends call me George."

The agents rode the elevator down with David, and walked with him to his car. During the short walk across the lot, both of the agents were constantly scoping around the surrounding area. The case had them both spooked. And they were worried for David. The young man was in danger of suffering severe physical or even more severe emotional trauma. Under the right circumstances fear and hope could be a dangerous cocktail.

BROGAN

Wayne Brogan was drunk. There was nothing unusual or special about that. What was unusual was that he was drunk in his own apartment. He'd been traveling so much lately, on the witch's errands, that he almost forgot what the place looked like. The forgetting was no great loss, his apartment was barely as nice as the worst of the lousy motels he encountered during his road trip, and way down in the cellar compared to the best. He was mildly irritated when he recalled that the high- end hotel he stayed in while in Vegas was on his own dime; actually, a whole lot of his own dimes. But that had been his decision.

Virtually every night he was on her quest he went to sleep thinking of her and that he would kill for the chance to nail her. Actually, upon further thought, he realized that was exactly what he'd done; he'd killed for the chance. And he'd gotten no indication that it would pay off for him. It pissed him off, but he still thought of her every night. And he knew that if she called, he wouldn't have the guts to tell her no. She had him hooked, and he knew a lot of it; maybe most of it was the way she could slip into his head at any time at all. He wouldn't even see her coming; and there she was; like another person in there talking to him, and telling him where to go and what to do. And he couldn't have said no, even if wanted to; which he didn't. He hadn't heard from her since she sent him to play Jack the Giant Killer; and almost gotten killed himself. No calls, no foreign thoughts in his head, nothing.

He'd gone through his money like shit through a goose. In the beginning it seemed like a bottomless pot. So much money he threw it around everywhere. He'd lost nearly twenty grand in Vegas; some before the night he put the screwdriver in the little sweetheart's ear, and some after. When he left the hotel, he had a plush white robe with the hotel's logo on it. That luxury alone had set him back a hundred dollars. At the time, it seemed like a good investment; the heat in his apartment was very undependable when it got really cold outside. But his back pack of cash was noticeably lighter when he got back than it had been when he left Boise for Vegas. He kept expecting a call from her, either by phone, or cerebrally, but nothing; no more work, no atta'boy! Nothing. But still he waited, and still he went to sleep thinking of her, and most nights dreaming of her.

BELADONNA

When Donna had first conceived of her mission, she was a well-known psychic, growing more powerful and more well-known at an astounding rate. Her increasing skills amazed even her. She had never doubted her power to develop her gifts till she would be unstoppable. The most common psychic ability, that of reaching people who have died, had become effortless. On occasion, just as a psychic exercise, she walked through a cemetery reading the names of long dead strangers, and probing in the other world for a psychic connection. Knowing nothing of the people she probed for, she asked who she'd contacted when she made a connection, just as one would ask who was on the other end of a phone call. Many of the spirits of the departed she contacted fought her probing; hesitant even in death to open up to an unknown interrogator. She thrived on the challenge they provided. She browbeat them, psychically imposing her force of will on them. She was training, as would an athlete preparing for a race, or a wrestling match. Her event would be coming soon. It would be the challenge that would be the measure of her skill, like a sprinter, straining to shatter a record. But there were no record books for the event in which she would be competing. There were no Psychic Olympics; no world championships: no gold medals. She had been building toward a goal far beyond anybody else's abilities or powers, or even comprehension. When it happened, everyone on the planet with even the slightest psychic ability would feel it. They wouldn't know what they felt. But they would know something unheard of and wonderful had occurred, and things had changed for all eternity. The human pawns she'd been manipulating at her whims were falling into place for checkmate. And it would be right soon. It was all she could do to contain her excitement. If she let her power get away from her, she could quite easily start exploding people's brains for no real reason except because she was able. Making the Fresno Detective's eyes pop from their sockets like corks from a bottle and gush brain matter from his skull was done for a purpose; to make Franklin Pace a suspect; and so, a distraction. And also, just to see if she could do it. Donna Grave felt the power building in her to a point she was afraid she might not be able to control it. And, in fact, she wasn't certain she wanted to control it. Thus far, every time she'd acted on impulse, things had turned out for the best. She had no compunction about sacrificing those necessary. But if people's heads start bursting like Roman candles it would be impossible not for someone to notice. But she was getting impatient. She knew impatient people get careless. But those were ordinary people. And she was moving farther beyond normal more every day. She was in control, and would stay in control.

At precisely ten pm her phone rang. There was no need to look at the caller ID. A broad smile crossed her face; at the same time satisfied and creepy. Her eyes began to glow an intense, fiery red. She picked up the phone and arranged what she was confident would be a decisive victory in the conflict she'd instigated. What she was planning would make the Japanese attack on Pearl Harbor look like a friendly pat on the back.

She knew it was not to be, but she thought it would be fun to produce a self-help video on how to grow from psychic to necromancer. She was sure it would be a best-seller, though most would view it as fiction. What she was striving for would keep her much too busy to write a book.

DAVID

David was very afraid. The case of stage fright he'd suffered the first time he stood before a crowd of people expecting him to entertain them was nothing compared to what overcame him as he hung up the phone. His appointment was set with the famed psychic. It was to be one at one am the second night after he'd called and made the appointment. He'd called her at ten pm on Saturday; so, the séance would take place at one am Tuesday morning. She had given only a few instructions; a dining room or sitting room with a largish center table and enough chairs to surround it with comfortable spacing. There were to be no open windows in the room, and no running air conditioner or fan to move drapes and so forth. Then, she asked how many people would be participating. "Well," he answered coolly, wondering if she wanted it to be a big production, or something more intimate. "It may be just you and me. Is that okay?"

"Of course," she purred seductively. David felt the skin crawl on the back of his neck. It wasn't an unpleasant feeling at all, and despite the fact that he'd been trying hard to concentrate on Patty and Davey, his mind instantly began envisioning far more personal interludes with the gorgeous psychic. He pushed his mind back to the arrangements.

"Wouldn't your mother like to join us? I understand she was the one who discovered your son was drowned."

"She probably would have, but unfortunately, she came down with a pretty bad case of food poisoning. She'll be enjoying the good life of lying back and watching TV till a nurse brings her meals, then fluffs her pillow, tucks her in, and makes sure she has a can of diet ginger ale, with a straw on her bedside table within easy reach."

"What a shame" Donna Grave purred, the sound bringing a response someplace other than the back of his neck, which made him think of Patty, and feel incredibly guilty. "I hope she'll be alright, and that her recovery will be both quick and comfortable. Please give her my best, and let her know that I'll be praying for her."

It was a beautiful gesture, and would be definite comfort if given under normal circumstances. But things were getting less and less normal. When she'd made the statement, the seductive purr still came through, but the words she said sounded a little hollow, like words spoken in a tiny room filled with cigar smoke. They were words coming from a mannequin, or an amateur actor, saying a line that he feels no strength in but says the line anyway because that's what he's expected to do. David thought for a minute. It might not be a bad idea to have some muscle here just in case. "Hey, the guys in the band were crazy about Davey. Before Patty died, we'd have a barbecue in the park once in a while, fix burgers and dogs. The guys would come over, joke and shoot the shit. I'd have the radio on to a good station. And the guys loved to play with Davey. They'd kick a soccer ball around, bounce balloons back and forth over a badminton net. Ed; our bass player (Stage name Dead) and our drummer Phil (stage name Swill) got to playing a game with Davey almost every time they saw him; they'd sit about ten feet apart on the grass. One of them would have Davey. He'd aim Davey in the right direction; toward the other guy and say 'go get him.' With some urging from his target Davey would charge along in his two-year-old's waddle (giggling all the way). Then he'd get turned around after some bouncing and tickling, and he was aimed back the way he'd come. And again, he ran/waddled all the way, giggling at the top of his tiny lungs. Patty said he was going to grow up thinking he was a wind-up-toy. David had said, "Let him laugh. There's no telling how life's going to go for him. When he has a chance to laugh good and hard, let him laugh. Sometimes when he gets to going like that, I got to laughing myself; laughing so hard I could barely get my breath, and I'm cryin' and rolling in the grass, and Davey jumped on me, and I pretended that he could hold me down. Then he'd usually get so excited that I'd have to stop and change a diaper."

Donna Grave had been listening intently to David's story. "I'll bet you didn't mind at all."

"Mind what at all? Changing the diapers? Nope I didn't mind a bit. I sure miss it."

This whole soliloquy, started by David describing the affection the other musicians felt toward Davey had led to a demonstration of a fathers love for his son. Even heard through the telephone the false sincerity was there, turned up full, and unmistakable. "Why don't you ask Dead and Swill to come over and sit in. Their friendship with Davey may make things go a little more smoothly. The dead recognize the presence of loved ones being around. It makes them feel secure and less shy about speaking"

"Good deal. I'll ask them to come by. I'll have the five Mil down payment with me. You know the rest of the deal."

"Yeah, I know". Her voice had changed. The seductive purr was now steely and all business. She had him hooked; now all she had to do was reel him in. That was one of her specialties.

In closing she said, "Well then, I'll see you at your mother's house. Tuesday morning at one, right?" Then she added as an afterthought, "I may come by about twelve, to get a few things ready, if that's okay?" David nodded like she could see him, and he had the uncomfortable sensation that perhaps she could. He said, "Right."

The way she was speaking it was almost impossible not to envision honey drooling from her mouth and dripping from her chin. When she said goodnight, the purr was back at full force. She added, "You take care. Be wary okay." It didn't sound like the common, friendly closing many people might say; "Be safe," maybe. To David it sounded like a warning, or possibly a thinly veiled threat. The purr, deep and seductive, was intended to gloss over the sting of the statement with a layer of overt sexuality.

PREPARATIONS

At noon on Monday, the day before the séance, John Paxton, George Alter, David Boyd and two of his band-mates, his bass player Ed, and drummer Phil were congregated in Paxton's office. Paxton took the floor first, "Ed, or do you prefer Dead?"

The musician answered, "Let's use Ed."

Paxton looked at Phil, and raised an eyebrow questioningly.

"Phil's fine."

"Good, that's easier to remember. Belladonna wants you two to sit in on the séance, right David?"

"Yeah, but's what with the Belladonna?

"Isn't that a poison?" Phil asked, and cringed a little.

Alter answered, "Yes, it comes from a plant called deadly nightshade. With her it started with something she said during a talk-show interview. She said her ex-husband called her Belladonna because living with her was killing him slowly, like a poison. She didn't offer any explanation, just kind of laughed it off. Of course, the press was all over it. The husband never answered any calls, and wouldn't talk about it."

David asked, "How long ago was that?"

Alter glanced at his notes. "Ten years."

"And he still won't talk, after ten years?"

"No and he never will. He died of a sudden brain aneurism five years ago."

Ed was wide-eyed. He let out a low whistle; barely more than a deep exhalation. Phil did a brief, but spot-on Twilight Zone trill; the familiar do-do, do-do, do-do, and then said, "You don't think this chick's really dangerous, do you?" Alter shrugged. "Probably not. The name just stuck in certain circles. If you say Belladonna to any cop, they'll know who you're talking about. "So," Paxton spoke up to break the tension. "Don't let it spook you. It's just a nick-name. She couldn't do any harm if she wanted to. The room where the séance will be held will be wired for sound and video. We'll see and hear everything that happens. I'll be in the upstairs bedroom, right at the top if the stairs." Paxton nodded at Alter. "George will be in the basement. We'll both be watching and listening. And there'll be a van full of agents three minutes away."

David had been silently taking everything in. "It sounds like you're doing everything possible to prevent me from reaching Davey."

Paxton had no answer. He really had unintentionally shifted his focus to what he wanted, and almost completely forgotten about what mattered to David. He had known David for years now, but had totally lost sight of what David was hoping for, and become focused solely on the murders. And at that point he had no answer. To say, "It's my job." wasn't sufficient justification. It would mean nothing to David; it would sound only like a hollow excuse. Paxton knew it would sound like that to David, because it sounded like that to him. The whole series of events leading up to what would be his first séance was very likely set in motion the night that David couldn't stand by and watch a young girl tortured and probably drowned. Since that event, David's life had been a roller coaster ride of small gains and huge losses; leading up to the loss of his child; the most terrible loss a parent can suffer.

David had gained Patty; the love of his life. Then, together he and Patty gained Danny. Then he lost Patty. And before he'd come close to coming to grips with that loss, he'd lost Danny. And as a side effect of that loss, his mother was a different person. She might never recover from feeling to blame for the boy's death. Then, almost despite his lack of interest, or caring, he'd become wealthy; the band more successful that he'd ever imagined.

And now, when the young man had glimpsed a glimmer of hope of reaching his boy, it must seem that all the FBI was doing was using him and his hope as a means to an end.

"David, you have my word; nobody will step in unless we see someone is in danger." Paxton looked at Alter, who nodded affirmation.

Alter said. "Promise. We may be hard-ass FBI agents, but nothing would make us happier than for you to reach Davey." David could see the truth in his eyes.

TIE-IN

George Alter heard the phone ringing from the shower. It was his cell. He usually laid it on the sink, within easy reach from the shower. But with all the time he'd been spending on what had become to be known within The Bureau as the death-metal-Killer Case, sleep had been scarce enough it was a miracle he could remember anything. The name was corny; like something from a made for TV movie. But it served the purpose. If the name ever got out to the press, they'd be short-stroking it for all it was worth. It seemed the press hadn't made a connection between the murders, which was a very good thing. Undue attention could scare away Donna Grave, or at least get her wind up. He got the impression she wouldn't scare easy. He hoped to get in a little rack time after his shower. He wrapped a towel around himself, trotted to the bedroom and got his phone from the nightstand. It was John Paxton. The first thing he said nearly knocked Alter from his feet; "We have a tie-in. The D.N.A. at the Fresno murder matched the unidentified perp David Boyd laid out with a bottle eight years ago.

BROGAN

At twelve a.m., twenty-five hours before the séance that he knew nothing about, Wayne Brogan came awake as though he'd been hit with an electric shock. He clutched his hands to his head like a child trying to drown out the sound of a parent's voice. But the voice he heard came not from outside of his head but from inside. The voice in his head this time wasn't as vague as, 'Go there and you'll know what to do.' This time the instructions were crystal clear; 'Go to Fresno, California and bring back Franklin Pace, no matter what it takes.'

PAXTON

Monday, at two p.m., eleven hours before the scheduled séance, John Paxton got a call notifying him that an unidentified man armed with a shotgun had entered the Fresno, California Police Headquarters, taken a receptionist and a hooker waiting to be booked hostage and forced the release of Franklin Pace. The two men had escaped in a Jeep Grand Cherokee after killing one officer and critically wounding another who attempted to stop them as they left the station. Witnesses said Pace didn't appear very happy about going with the man, and appeared practically pleased to be dragged to the waiting Jeep.

BELADONNA

Donna looked at her reflection in a full-length mirror, and was pleased with the image looking back. She wanted to look her best. This would be a very special night for her.

She was every bit as enthusiastic about the prospect of reaching David Boyd's dead son as he was; but for very different reasons. She'd tried to reach the boy on her own, but had been unsuccessful. She'd come to believe after all the years she'd spent honing her talents that how easy it was to reach someone who had passed over might depend on her motives. It was as if the person she was trying to reach could see into her, the way she could see into others. She'd chosen David Boyd and his son for her plan because she personally believed that the sins of the father _are_ visited upon the son. At least she hoped so. Donna was her own one-woman cult. She studied the Bible, and picked and chose verses that suited her. She was counting on this verse. In this case, the father had spent years preaching hate and death from stages every Friday and Saturday night, and sometimes Sunday.

In fact, she had no reason to believe the Boyd kid was destined for hell. But that didn't mean she couldn't use him as a key to get her foot in the door.

HOSTILE TAKEOVER

As promised, Donna Grave rang the doorbell at David's mother's house at midnight. John Paxton was already in the upstairs bedroom. George Alter was in the basement. After considerable consideration, David had chosen the dining room, as it most closely suited Donna's requests. The space was completely covered by cameras and microphones secreted around the room. Paxton had personally overseen the procedure. After repeated prodding, the technician, who was getting irritated at being hovered over, assured him that the microphones would pick up the softest mouse fart that might occur within thirty feet of the room.

David nervously escorted the psychic into the room.

"Will this be okay?" he asked in a reverent whisper.

David had found out what he could about her on the internet, including dozens of pictures, but was still stunned by her beauty. She was truly striking.

David hadn't been there to hear Eddie Dean, the tip-line volunteer, describe her as she'd appeared in his dream. Only Franklin Pace and the unfortunate Detective Cray had been there. Like Eddie Dean, he was most astounded by her eyes; green as an emerald lit from within. David instantly got the chilling impression that she could see through him. It scared him, because he was afraid she would see him thinking about the FBI agents that were all around them. He didn't know if a psychic was the same thing as a mind reader. If that happened, she wouldn't let him talk to Davey. That was all he really wanted. He wanted to know who had held his little boy under water.

David had never killed a monster before, but he'd love nothing more than to get the chance. The closer the séance had gotten the more he wanted revenge. His primary motive, by far, was to see if Davey was at peace. He'd lost his mother before he really got a chance to know her, or to know the love she felt for him. Then he'd died at two at the hands of some psychopath. The boy had suffered enough in his short life. David would like to believe he was at peace now. Identifying the killer would be a fringe benefit. David had decided that if he got his hands on the killer, he could happily turn the violence he sang about into reality.

David was worried about whether a psychic could read minds. He had no clue what Donna Grave had morphed into, like a perverted butterfly or moth emerging from a cocoon. And he had no idea of the motive behind her offer to try to reach Davey. After carefully looking around the room she pronounced it suitable for her needs. Smiling sweetly, she asked David if she might have a glass of water. He excused himself and left the room. When he returned with her water after only a few minutes, the table was covered with a woven tapestry the color of storm clouds, that he hadn't seen her carrying when she got there. The uneasy sensation he'd felt since her arrival grew more intense. He wondered if the agents had observed her slight-of-hand on their monitors. He was torn between his need to contact Davey and his growing fear. And his anger was intensifying with astonishing speed. It was occupying the forefront of his emotions more by the minute. It almost overwhelmed the grief he'd felt since losing his wife and child. There was nothing he could do to the truck driver that had taken Patty from him, but he could put a bullet or a knife in the person who'd killed Davey, or more appropriately, hold him under water till his lungs burned and filled with water, and his eyes bulged in their sockets. He was shocked by the pent-up fury in him, but felt no shame at it.

As one a.m. neared, the psychic had him call his two bandmates in from where they'd been waiting in the narrow front hallway and they took seats around the table. At her instructions, David turned off all the lights in the room except one lamp. The gloom made David even more uneasy. Ed and Phil sat on either side of him, and he could sense the tension that filled the room; everywhere except from across the table where Donna Grave sat.

David sat with his eyes mostly downcast but occasionally glanced furtively up at the psychic. He'd had no idea what to expect from her, but definitely didn't expect her to sit motionless in a virtually dark room. Finally, at a few minutes past one she said, "David." Her voice took him so by surprise that he jumped. So did the musicians on either side of him. He looked at her guiltily, and said, "I'm sorry." "Don't be," she said. "I'm sorry I startled you." She sounded honestly apologetic, almost motherly. Still, he felt like she was an actress playing the part of someone who cared about him. They sat, silent and still for another five minutes. Then Phil, who David had known was getting twitchy from inactivity asked, "What now?" Donna looked slowly and deliberately from one of them to the other, around the table. Then her eyes settled on David. "David, what would you like?"

"I want to talk to Davey," David answered, impatience lending an edge to his voice. "And what do you want to say to Davey?" She was purring again. Ed cleared his throat loudly. "I want to know if he's at peace. I want him to know I miss him, and I love him."

Now it was she who was becoming impatient, and it was clear in her voice. "Is that all you want to say to him?"

"No; I want to know who murdered him."

In the bedroom over their heads, and in the basement beneath them, the agents' hands instinctively moved to their guns. They had no idea what to expect in response to David's statement, delivered bluntly, and without hesitation. Beneath the circular table, where the séance had not yet commenced Ed; Corpse Whisperer's bass player, always the mellowest of the group, clicked the heels of his boots sharply together. There was a very soft 'sprong' sound, metallic and as soft as a whisper, from the vicinity of his feet. David's reflexes were very fast. He ducked his head quickly to see a six-inch-long stiletto protruding from each of the boot's toes. He made a small angry sound in Ed's direction. Ed mouthed the word Sorry. He was sorry if that little swish was heard, but not that he'd brought the hidden shoe weapons. Now he felt marginally safer. He'd been stunned that the Psychic arrived with no visible bodyguards. They'd shown up in a fourteen-foot-long silver colored Cadillac limo. David was shocked to see Ed and Phil on board. The psychic had picked them up for the ride. It also gave her time to become more comfortable with their life force. From outside it had looked like there was more room to hide in that rolling monster than in the house they were now in.

Phil had stooped slightly, staring at a street light reflecting in one of the behemoth's windows. He saw several coronas of slightly different colored layers of glass arcing across the window. He tapped it discretely with a fingertip and whispered to David, "Bulletproof." David's anxiety level had immediately multiplied at light speed by a factor of at least five. He only wished his intelligence was sufficient to process events rapidly enough for him to be able to wrap his mind around what was happening. The memories he'd packed securely away for hours of peering upon at some more suitable time and place, and with proper reverence crashed in on him, nearly debilitating. They were a distraction he didn't need at present. The three musicians had stood beside the limo, like mechanical figures whose springs had wound down. Then the psychic had asked, are we going to stand here till dawn." She sounded less than friendly.

"No, let's go in." David had answered shakily. He began walking toward his mother's house; worrying as he walked that the psychic would hear his knees knocking. Though he was in the lead physically, there was no doubt about who was in charge. It was time for what he'd wanted so desperately; namely a séance. As they entered the house, David paused and picked up a duffel bag and handed it to Donna. He said, "There's the down payment. Do you want to count it?" Donna looked at the bag, as though she could see right through the heavy canvas, and said, "No I trust you."

Other than the inexplicably appearing tapestry which had seemingly materialized out of thin air, nothing had changed within the dining room; no glowing crystal ball; no black cat. All of his mother's furniture sat right where it always did.

SEANCE

David's mind returned to the present. Surprisingly, sitting in the gloom of his mother's dining room, and replaying the psychic's arrival in his mind had made him more than a little drowsy. He looked up at the psychic expectantly. She wore a smile, humorless but satisfied. She had wanted him drowsy, and was serene in the knowledge that she was in control. Ed, always the impatient one, said, "Don't they call people like you Mediums?" Donna nodded. "Some do. Or Spiritualists. The name is unimportant. The ability is what matters." Suddenly her eyes opened impossibly wide. In an instant the jade green of cat's eyes turned a burning red. The burning appearance was more than illusion. The unmistakable smell of heat filled the room and the temperature near her rose dramatically. It was like being near an old-fashioned radiator in a house where the thermostat was turned all the way up.

Without warning she lowered her head till her forehead touched the table. It wasn't done rapidly, and made no sound when it happened. In moments, the tapestry began to smolder where it was only inches from her fiery eyes. David thought of the Superman TV shows, where the hero used his x-ray vision to superheat something. Ed thought of old sci-fi movies about aliens with death rays in their eyes. Phil thought of nothing but being gone.

He suddenly jumped up, so suddenly the chair tipped over behind him and clattered to the floor. He ran toward the door. As he rushed past David, he looked at him and gasped, "I'm sorry!" Donna lifted her head, her glowing gaze following him as he went. Phil reached the doorway that opened on the hall leading straight to the front door. He was suddenly stopped dead by a fist to his chest. To his credit, Phil didn't go down. And he didn't turn and run toward the door that opened on the kitchen. He took a swing at the total stranger who'd hit him.

Wayne Brogan stood in the doorway, grinning madly and wobbling on his feet. Phil's punch didn't connect. It wouldn't have mattered if it did. Phil wasn't a big man, and Wayne Brogan was. Brogan was wobbling because, like always, he was drunk. A second, smaller man that none of the musicians knew stood in the hall behind Brogan. He was crouched, trying to hide behind the bigger man. David and his friends caused no fear in the stranger; it was his best client that terrified him. As casually as if he were swatting a mosquito, Brogan back-handed Phil, sending him crashing to the floor on his back. When David could pull his eyes away from Phil, he looked up and recognized Brogan as the man who'd been trying to drown Patty years before in the hotel bathroom.

Donna Grave appeared to have lost interest in what was happening in the room. She'd closed her eyes tightly and was muttering something under her breath. Ed stared at her, transfixed by the red glow showing brightly through her eyelids. But David jumped up, knocking his chair over as Phil had his. Wayne Brogan looked at him, fluttered his eyelids with their hideous pentagram tattoos, and said, "How's the boy, rock star?" David grabbed Phil's overturned chair and flung it at Brogan with all his strength. The chair connected where Phil's punch hadn't. Through sheer luck, one of the chair's legs hit Brogan in the center of his forehead. The big man staggered back into Franklin Pace, who still cowered behind him.

Through all of this, Donna Grave sat at the table, her eyes closed, muttering quietly but intently, seemingly oblivious to the mayhem around her. Reaching behind himself, Wayne Brogan grabbed Franklin Pace by the neck and, using him as a human cane righted himself from David's blow with the chair. Pace issued a desperate choking noise and batted at Brogan's arms with both hands. The slaps had no effect whatsoever, and Pace's face turned red. His eyes bulged like overfilled balloons. Slowly, and deliberately Wayne Brogan reached in his pocket and brought out a revolver. He raised it and pointed it at David, at the same time pushing Franklin Pace away like so much garbage. Donna's agent hit the wall in the hallway, and slid to the floor. Brogan again looked at David. "Blindside me with a bottle, will ya?" He thumbed back the hammer. The loud click was barely discernible over the continued mumbling from the psychic. The sound she made was getting no louder, but seemed to be growing in urgency; her voice getting deeper and more husky, almost a growl. David winced, expecting a bullet at any second. There was the roar of a gun, sounding like a thunder-clap in the close quarters, but the pain David was expecting didn't happen. A hole appeared in Wayne Brogan's chest. The cloth of his shirt, as well as the ragged edges of the flesh around the hole were flared out in the direction of the dining room; the location of the abbreviated séance. David heard the faint whine of the bullet whizzing past, and heard it hit the wall behind him. Brogan fell forward; face down on the carpet. In the hallway, behind the spot where Brogan had been while taking aim at David, Special Agent George Alter stood; his stance wide, both hands holding a pistol with tendrils of smoke rising from its muzzle.

Through all that was happening, Donna Grave sat at the table, her eyes closed, and the sound of words spoken only half-aloud coming from her open mouth.

Franklin Pace lay on the floor, curled in a fetal position, babbling incoherently, making sounds that were more moans than words. Alter asked, "David, are you alright?" Then he stepped over Franklin Pace and took a few steps into the room. Unbelievably, when Alter was only a few feet from him, Wayne Brogan rolled over, and shot him in the chest. Alter pitched forward, falling on top of Brogan, twice squeezing the trigger of his own gun as he fell. Brogan's forehead exploded, shattered by the bullet, as did the back of his skull. Before he died, he looked up at Donna Grave and asked, "Did I do good?"

The psychic laughed aloud. "That's enough!" Paxton's voice came from the doorway. David had never heard such rage in a voice. Donna didn't stop laughing wildly. She sounded as demented as Paxton did furious.

Ed still sat in his chair; his hands locked in a death grip on the table's edge. He had the dazed expression of a man whose reality had taken an unexpected ninety-degree turn. David had taken a step toward Brogan when he hit the floor. He stood balanced on one foot, with the other folded back, cocked to deliver a kick to Brogan's head. But when George Alter fell on top of the insane animal, David held the blow. In David's current state of fury, Brogan's mangled head would probably have disintegrated. That wasn't the reason for him stopping the kick; he couldn't have cared less about the state of Brogan's skull, dead or alive. He feared hitting George Alter. He didn't know if the agent still lived, but couldn't take the risk.

CONFESSION-MOTIVES

Special Agent John Paxton took a step forward. Franklin Pace still cowered in the corner where it met the floor. He made a grab at the detective's ankle. Paxton turned only enough to look at Pace, but didn't study him for long before walking toward the psychic, dragging Pace behind him. Finally tiring of the extra worthless load, he fired a shot into the floor leaving a short stub of flesh and bone where Pace's left thumb had been. Pace immediately let go, and lay where he was; his arms wrapped around his head. Paxton strode onward, directly toward the psychic. The whole time, she had rambled on; grunting sounds intertwined with unexpected legible words. David leaned closer, and strained to listen. It brought to mind the fictional Klingon language he'd heard in countless Star Trek episodes. Through the sounds they could hear her panting like a dog. She mostly said, "Come on, when!? Then, "Tell me when, god damn it!" I need to know! I deserve to know!" She wasn't looking to get something tangible. It was information she wanted. Paxton slowly walked to David, where he stood astounded by what he'd seen.

Paxton asked, "David, are you alright?"

David nodded weakly. Glad to be alive, David shook in terror at Donna's glance. The red heat in her eyes had overflowed, and now her whole forehead was beet red, and her cheeks were becoming more crimson with each passing second. Also, with each passing second David, Ed, and Paxton were more scared that with every heavy breath she blew out she would begin breathing fire, like a movie dragon. The heat had to be building in her, and must eventually find an escape. Each exhalation made a shrill teakettle-like whistling noise that thankfully, at least for a moment, drowned out her unnerving incoherent mumbling.

"Check on George!" Paxton snapped at Ed. Ed ran to where the fallen agent lay atop Wayne Brogan. He had no idea what he should do, so he pressed his fingers against the side of Alter's neck like they did on TV. He looked up at Paxton and shook his head. Pushed to the breaking point, Paxton raised his weapon and fired. The bullet grazed the side of Donna Grave's neck and shattered the plaster of the wall behind her. She showed no response; just kept on babbling. Paxton shouted, "Hey bitch! The next one goes between your eyes!" She turned to face Paxton, and some of the fire in her eyes dimmed. David felt certain she had intentionally dialed back her flames, just as he would with an amplifier. She wanted to talk, and wanted to be listened to, not feared, at least for the moment.

"Agent Paxton, I presume. You've been looking for me, looking hard, I think. But you hadn't found me till now. And that was only because I let you find me." She was gloating, and enjoying it. "I killed three people, no, wait, four if you include the detective in Fresno, and you couldn't find me. And here we are! David and I are going to talk to Davey. And you can share in the experience; how lucky you are!"

David was dazed; floored by her mention of Davey. "What?" The single word was all he could manage.

"You sentimental fool. I'm not here for you. I'm here for me. I'm going to talk to Davey myself. I don't care what you do. I have a question for him. I went to a lot of trouble to talk to him. I killed him so I could ask him a question."

David recalled her mumbling, "When? I need to know when." She had asked the question aloud, over and over. If she'd gotten an answer, it was heard only by her. David charged at her. Paxton watched, gun in hand, waiting and hoping David would strangle the life out of her. Cop or not, there was no way he'd lift a finger to stop him.

Before David could reach Donna, Franklin Pace started screaming from the hallway where Paxton had performed 9mm thumb amputation surgery. Distracted by the sound, David stopped short of the psychic, arms outstretched, and hands open to grab her throat.

Franklin Pace dragged himself through the doorway into the dining room. The flow of blood from his hand had all but stopped. His heart couldn't keep up; blood was gushing from his eye sockets and his ears in steady streams.

Donna looked at Agent Paxton and said, "Now I've killed five." She paused, and then made an off-hand motion toward George Alter. "Six, if you include him." Ed pulled his hand away from Alter's neck, and issued a small shriek, as though he'd briefly forgotten what he was doing.

"Why?" David screamed, the sound of his own voice startling him.

"At the risk of sounding like a movie villain who explains things just before being caught, I think a little gloating is in order. And I have, or rather you, have proven your inability to stop me." She faced David. "In answer to your question; "There is something only the dead can tell me. And after a little homework I concluded that your son would be the perfect dead person to ask. But of course, he wasn't dead." Paxton took a step closer to her, and pulled back the slide on his gun, chambering a round to replace the one he'd used to blow off Franklin Pace's thumb. He readjusted his aim, making sure Donna saw him doing so. "So, you killed him; and two others." he said. Donna looked him in the eyes, measuring his willingness to kill her. She didn't like what she saw. When she continued her tone had changed; less arrogant, and not so confident. "I didn't really kill anyone, you know. He did." She pointed at Wayne Brogan.

"That isn't going to make you any less dead if I put a bullet in you. Or I might just save my bullet till I see what's left of you after David's done with you." He used his gun to wave David on. David crossed the space that separated them in two seconds, and grabbed the psychic's throat. He began shaking her, and screamed, "Why?"

"It's time for a changing of the guard," she said, remarkably calm, her voice altered only slightly by David's assault. "A hostile takeover, you could say." Though being choked, she offered a sly smile, as though she was sharing a clever secret. "There's nobody who can't be replaced." David intensified the shaking.

"What did my son do to you?"

"Not a thing."

"And the others?" Paxton asked.

"Oh, they were merely a diversion, to make you focus less on David and his boy. There's nothing like a good serial killer to monopolize law enforcement's time and attention."

She was bragging; relishing having the upper hand. "Davey was the only one I cared about. She sneered at David. "With your history of dragging humanity into an abyss on stage, I knew he was the perfect one. Even you had no idea how much damage you'd done. Bootlegs of your music were all over Europe years ago. You've helped push hundreds of people over the edge. Maybe thousands." Thousands who believed you; almost worshiped you.

David was crying. Tears flew from his eyes as he shook Donna. "So, I made Davey the perfect one for what?"

When she answered, David was so stunned he stopped shaking her. "To tell me when the end of days will occur."

"What?"

"When Hell will be ripe for a hostile takeover. Like I said, there's nobody who can't be replaced." She continued, as though addressing an auditorium full of people at a self-help seminar. "Over a trillion people have died since the Earth came into being. If only half of those souls are in hell, that's a huge population just waiting for a new leader. Better to lead in Hell than to serve in Heaven."

Paxton stepped closer yet, and pressed the muzzle of his pistol against her temple. "Why did you kill Davey Boyd?" From behind him came a voice from the dead.

"She's a necromancer."

Paxton and David both turned, but David didn't release his grip. George Alter looked from one of them to the other. Ed crawled backwards into a corner, afraid he'd seen a ghost, and supremely glad he'd been wrong when he checked for a pulse.

"A necromancer; she's a wizard." Alter continued, blood seeping over his lips. "She communicates with the dead to foresee the future." He grimaced with pain. Then he smiled slightly, his bloody lips looking like they were colored with lipstick. Donna Grave stared at Alter, stunned as much by his knowledge of her real self as by him being alive. George smiled a bloody, thin lipped, but satisfied smile at her and said, "Google; go figure'. "She wants Davey to tell her when the world will end, so she can mount a coup, and take over Hell."

Paxton yelled, "I'll be happy to send you there, but you'll be on your own campaigning."

He squeezed the trigger twice in quick succession. The shots filled the room with false thunder. The loud crashes of sound were filtered through by the almost musical tones of the bones from Donna Grave's frontal cortex peppering the front sounding-board of Mom's old piano. Some of the smallest, and fastest moving fragments punched through the board, hitting the strings, and making a twisted serious of notes, that as they faded mysteriously became both relaxing and chilling. Then, as a result of being stricken by Paxton's bullet continuing through the doomed piano, the lid support shattered into twigs, and the lid slammed down with the finality of a coffin lid. The piano was one more victim of the melee in the dining room. Phil had slapped himself hard a dozen times and appeared to have his shit mostly together. A few twitches still showed here and there, but he was better.

Things went quiet. "As still as a cemetery in winter", Phil offered, to break the chilling silence, his voice still trembling slightly. That statement soothed no one's nerves.

As the quiet stretched out, they were beginning to believe it was over. Donna said, "I'm not done yet." She was angry, undaunted by her mangled head. Her brain was visible through the shattered front of her skull. One eye was punched so far back in her head, it would have been invisible if not for the fierce fire burning in it. David remembered his earlier analogy; like staring into a window at Hell. Her other eye lay on her cheek, hanging from the whisper-thin strands of the optic nerve. Still, the eye glowed. In a move so quick and unexpected, that David let go a brief but searing scream; Belladonna shifted her gaze to David. Determination showed on her ruined, blood-soaked face. Then the house began to tremble. Slightly at first, but quickly growing till it seemed the house was in a super-sized industrial model cement mixer. The agents and musicians were thrown around the room. Still, the chair Donna sat in stayed upright and still. Just before the house ceased shaking the wall behind her and much of the ceiling collapsed on and around the Necromancer. She really was a strong bitch: immediately pushing debris off of her in miniature landslides of wood and plaster. When the house stopped shaking it was tilted, like a room or hallway in a carnival funhouse. Paxton looked out a window at the street beyond and its straight, orderly line of streetlights. The lights were lower than they should be, like the poles had been shortened. He looked out a different window, and the trees on that side of the house also appeared to have been shortened. He realized the house was hanging in the air, levitating ten feet above its foundation, like something on a David Copperfield TV special. It hung there for twenty seconds. Then, as though a giant hand which was holding it let go, the house dropped straight down, landing on the foundation close enough to its original position to prevent it from breaking into a dozen large pieces, or into thousands of pieces of shrapnel. Cracks shot across the floors, and wide chunks of plaster fell from the walls. The chandelier fell from the ceiling and crashed onto the table they'd been seated around. Everyone jumped with surprise except Donna, who now, at least in Paxton's mind, was Belladonna. She sat, still and regal. The room they were in had stayed, for the most part, intact. The surprisingly undead George Alter pushed himself off of the definitely dead Wayne Brogan. Ed helped him sit up. With Ed's support on one side and Phil's support on the other, George was moved to where he could sit leaning against one of the walls. Ed tore off the bottom foot of his t shirt and folded it into a thick pad and pressed it tightly against the hole in Alter's chest. Phil put his own belt and Alter's together and pulled them snug around his chest to hold the pad in place. Paxton, Alter, and the three musicians sat in a row along the wall, waiting; for what, they didn't know. Franklin Pace had struggled his way behind a high-backed sofa and was doing his best to be invisible, peeking out at Donna Grave once in a while.

Everything was quiet, but Phil made no unnerving comparisons. They spoke only in muted whispers, not wishing to attract Belladonna's attention.

The ill-fated séance had commenced at 1a.m. A glance at Paxton's watch showed it to be four-thirty-seven a.m. Donna showed she had somehow conjured a blue velvet tapestry that was now draped regally over her shoulders. While she was conjuring, she'd apparently conjured a plastic surgeon. Unless she was making them hallucinate, she now had a third eye in the center of her forehead, very near the huge damage done by Paxton's bullet. Her normal, beautiful eyes had returned to their common cool jade color, and were partway closed, as if she was fighting sleep. Thankfully the new eye was also closed. None of them cared to see what was behind the lid.

She had again taken up mumbling, although now the mumbling was mixed with a chant; louder and more insistent. Still, she kept asking, over and over, "When? When will it be?" Over and over the same thing; "When?" Finally, the chanting turned to screaming. "When will it be? "When?" "When, damn you Tell me when!!" The last was yelled, at the top of her lungs, her voice breaking, as blood sprayed from her mouth from her fractured vocal-chords. It was meant as a command, not a request.

Before her shout faded from the room, the house again shook. Every bit as bad as before, but differently. Instead of an earthquake-like shake, it was like a disturbance began at one end of the house and moved its length to the other. They could feel the floor ripple as it passed. It felt like there was something alive moving around beneath them. Then whatever had occurred was repeated in the opposite direction.

Special Agent Paxton, trained by years of dealing with the unexpected and unexplainable was the one whose mind envisioned the closest thing to the truth. He felt it was like something alive down there was looking for the right place to come through. All the while, the two agents and three musicians kept control of their bodies as much as possible. Behind the sofa, Franklin Pace, barely a husk, empty of blood and brain matter, flopped around like a rag doll.

Through it all Donna Grave sat stone still in the dining room chair; not a hair out of place; not a tear track through her mascara. No sign of a chipped nail from holding on to the chair arms. As the rolling stopped, and the house sat still, she crowed like a bird that had snatched up something in its mangling claws. It was the same image that appeared in the heads of the scared human occupants of the room.

Then the impossible happened. The far end of the house from where they'd held the séance exploded upward. There was no smoke or flame. It was no man-made act. There was only one way it could have happened; something had come up out of the ground in a damn big rush. And the house had been in the way.

As the men watched, a cloud of boards, pipes, plaster, fixtures and appliances was thrown skyward. A washing machine barely missed landing on David as it fell back down. It was clear that something was coming up, from the ground under the house. Something huge. Something being born of the earth below. And judging by its sounds, it was pissed. Finally, in one huge lurch it was born. It rose to its full height. Broken, burning lumber clung to its rough, leathery-appearing hide. The aster of Hell as they all knew it must be, was easily thirty feet tall, stood on two legs, had long arms, and clawed hands. It had the head and horns of a bull or ram, with one huge center eye, which burned with fire, as it pawed at the broken ground with mammoth cloven hoofs. A long, thick tail dragged behind it. The Master of Hell turned all ways, scanning the area of carnage, blinking its one eye, looking carefully for something or somebody. Its gaze stopped on Donna Grave, and examined her carefully, before stepping closer to where she sat in her mock throne. Possibly her sensitive intuition clued her in to what was going to happen, or she simply saw the huge foot lift into the air. Either way she didn't or couldn't act quickly enough.

Remarkably fast, a gigantic clawed foot trailing tendrils of flame and smoke came down on Donna Grave and her makeshift throne and crushed her into the ground below the smashed floor, grinding her in the dirt like a cigarette butt.

For the first time, David heard Davey. Clear as a bell, and as sweet as honey he heard his boy say "Love-oo-Daddy". Then Davey laughed, long and true, and David laughed with him. Then he was gone. The burning monster was gone. Belladonna was gone. The edges of the shattered wood she'd been driven through burned like the deep red char of a burning charcoal briquette. What remained were three musicians, whose thoughts about death and Hell were changed forever, and two FBI Agents sitting in the rubble of David's mother's house. The three musicians picked up the few unbroken chairs and sat to wait for the authorities to arrive, as they surely would. They helped George into one of them. Phil sat next to George, keeping pressure on the wound with a piece of Donna Grave's tapestry till the paramedics got there and took over. There would be time to practice their stories later. They knew nobody would believe the truth. Two of them being FBI Special Agents would help. Wayne Brogan's body was a mass of deep-purple bruises, and some of his bones didn't seem to conform to the physical norm; many seeming to have inherited a new elbow or knee here and there, making a bone shoot off at a crazy angle. Franklin Pace was a dried-up scarecrow. Donna Grave's disappearance might never be solved. Paxton asked of no one in particular, "Wonder what that was all about?" George Alter said, with a confused shrug, "I guess the CEO of Hell wasn't ready to be pushed from a job he's been doing so long."

Ed nodded. "Makes sense to me."

EPILOGUE

Upon arriving at the heap of rubble that had been David Boyd's mother's house, the first responders; police and fire fighters were stunned to find five people alive just a dozen yards from the center of whatever had happened.

At first glance, it appeared the mayhem could only have been the result of an explosion beneath the ground the house had set on. The neighborhood was built on a maze of natural gas lines. Still, upon examination there was no evidence of the fireball that would accompany an underground gas explosion. Amazingly, the five survivors; one with a gunshot wound, had been missed by the worst of the upheaval; which is how it was described in the final investigation's report. It appeared to have been centered under a section of the house some distance of rooms from where they were found. The floor of the room where they were found was crooked, and was a wreck of splintered wood, as though something had crashed down through it.

The five survivors of the séance knew what had come up from the ground beneath the house, and what had smashed down through the floor; a large smoking foot, squashing a would-be pretender to a throne most people wouldn't believe existed.

An investigation of the site found no concrete evidence of an explosion. But the entire neighborhood was saturated with a sulfuric smell like that which follows the blowing out of a match.

Within six months, every home in a five-block radius of the wrecked house was vacant. Most had for-sale signs out front, but nobody would buy them for the same reason the owners were selling; the stench. Also, rumors arose about what had happened there, and most, in some way involved the supernatural or even Satanism. The people leaving blamed the stench, but in truth, they were frightened.

David bought his mother a small house in the tiny town of Crossbow, which sat on an island off the Georgia coast; as far away from Boise as possible. It's peaceful, and she planted a garden, where she works many mornings to hopefully come to grips with the guilt feelings she still carries over Davey's death.

'Corpse Whisperer' became 'Whisperer' and played southern rock, sometimes in clubs with moose heads and wagon wheels on the walls.

Special Agent Alter eventually returned to duty, but during his recuperation period he spent a great deal of time researching Necromancers; not just on-line but in many very old, and obscure books. He told David that the reason Belladonna hadn't been able to reach Davey was because he wasn't in Hell. David said he already knew that. He never forgot the brief but definitely real words he heard Davey speak to him, and the way he laughed.

Special Agent Paxton and Special Agent Alter went on investigating far less unique and challenging cases than the one involving David Boyd and Belladonna; with Paxton frequently lamenting the lack of challenge in the more common-place cases, than apprehending the Necromancer had entailed. He said he missed the action. Alter immediately said, "Be careful what you wish for: or you might just get it."

Hell still exists. Sadly, that will never change. But Belladonna isn't in charge there. She would have found a way to make it worse.

THE END

ABOUT THIS BOOK:

In 2015 I published the book "**NECROMANCER.**" The book received really good reviews but in following up on it, I became aware of some formatting issues. I had also deleted quite a bit of text to keep the book at a reasonable length, and make it an easier read. I know many readers are hesitant to take on a big book. This book has much of that text added back in to make the story more complete, and the corrections made. I even made a new cover. Thanks for reading!

Eddie Roy

www.ingramcontent.com/pod-product-compliance
Lightning Source LLC
Chambersburg PA
CBHW031409310726
48971CB00003B/800